MEET ME at the INTERSECTION

Edited by
REBECCA LIM & AMBELIN KWAYMULLINA

 FREMANTLE PRESS

Contents

Ambelin Kwaymullina, *Voices from the Intersections,* 2018.
gouache on paper, 395 x 255 mm

Cover Artwork

The front cover artwork is extracted from Ambelin Kwaymullina's painting *Voices from the Intersections*. A colour reproduction of the whole artwork is on the back cover.

The circles are the voices of marginalised peoples in Australia, beginning in the centre with the voices of the First Peoples and flowing out from there to other marginalised peoples in this land.

The white shapes are the intersections of different forms of exclusion that seek to silence marginalised peoples. These intersections are also meeting places where we share our experiences with each other and reach out to the wider society.

The blue that surrounds the circles and intersections represents our strength. Like water, we find a way, flowing around and between the intersections of exclusion to speak our stories.

The rainbow colours are the beauty, complexity and diversity our voices bring to the world.

Introduction

Rebecca Lim
(migrant Chinese Australian) and
Ambelin Kwaymullina (Palyku)

This is a book of 'Own Voices'* stories — stories about marginalised peoples told *by* people from those marginalised groups. The genesis of this collection was conversations across 2015 and 2016 where the two of us shared our frustration at the massive under-representation of diverse Australian voices in children's and young adult (YA) literature and the lack of a formal movement in Australia to focus attention on, and tackle, systemic bias — or what we like to call *problems with the filter*.

We decided to do something about it. So we founded *Voices from the Intersection* in 2016 — a purely volunteer

* This term was first coined by author Corinne Duyvis as a way of referring to stories about diverse characters written by authors from that same diverse group.

initiative with no funding or resources other than ourselves, our time, and our contacts across the writing and publishing industries.

Voices aims to support the creation of Own Voice stories through establishing publication and mentorship opportunities for emerging YA and children's writers, illustrators and publishing professionals who are First Nations, People of Colour, LGBTIQA+ or living with disability.

After successfully holding our inaugural publisher pitch day for almost forty emerging marginalised creators (writers and illustrators) in March 2017, we reached out to our contacts in publishing with the idea of creating an Own Voices collection for young adults.

The wonderful Fremantle Press embraced the anthology with enthusiasm. We were soon joined by a host of fiercely talented emerging and published writers from a spectrum of diverse and intersectional backgrounds. We were not surprised at the urgency and energy of the voices — for we knew the stories were out there. But even we couldn't have anticipated the degree to which we were awed and inspired by the tales in this anthology. To sit with these stories was to sit amongst stars; every one shining a light on to different experiences, and each a point of insight into the diversity — which is to say, the strength and truth — of Australia and its peoples.

Although we have put the stories in this anthology into

groups, we recognise the impossibility of confining these narratives, many of which speak to multiple aspects of identities and experiences. We are each enriched by our experiences but greater than our exclusion. Gathering stories into groups provides an entry point into the narratives, but once you enter the narratives themselves, you will find yourself in worlds that cannot be reduced to labels.

Our collection starts with the cover. This is Ambelin's contribution: a painting which tells the tale of this anthology — the strength of diverse voices, the links we make with each other; and the intersections of oppression that prevent us being heard. But these intersections can also be points of connection as we reach out to each other and the world to share our stories. Some of the intersections present in this anthology are mapped in this Introduction, but we don't presume to know them all. We hope that the readers of this collection will be inspired by both the experiences that are like their own and the ones that are not. We hope that they will reflect upon the many intersections within this book, and find their own points of connection with the stories told.

We begin the written contributions to this collection in the same way that Australia began — with the stories of First Nations peoples. Ellen van Neerven (Yugambeh) writes of dreams and football, of the complexities of being Black and Queer, and of fighting for your future. Graham Akhurst (Kokomini) speaks in poetry of culture and resilience, the terror of colonisation and the great strength of First Peoples. Kyle Lynch (Wongi) writes memoir, a story told through dialogue of his search for a job that offers a powerful insight into life, hope and family in the Kurrawang Aboriginal Christian Community. Ezekiel Kwaymullina (Palyku) tells of being Aboriginal, dyslexic, and ignored, by the teachers supposed to teach him to read.

Ezekiel's story offers a point of connection with the next group of stories in the anthology: those of Australians living with a disability. Olivia Muscat relates the experience of losing her sight, a vanishing of written words and a changing of worlds. Chinese-Australian writer Mimi Lee tells of culture, family and coming to terms with mental illness. Jessica Walton writes a poignant tale of finding connections from the perspective of a character who is (like her) Queer and living with the phantom pain of a missing limb.

This brings us to stories from LGBTIQA+ writers that speak through time and space. Kelly Gardiner sets her tale in the 1950s, writing of the meeting of young Queer women against a backdrop of espressos, Frank Sinatra and motorbikes. Jordi Kerr pens a magical speculative fiction tale of difference and acceptance in rural Australia. Yvette Walker reaches through time to provide comfort and wisdom to her younger self. Melanie Rodriga writes about assembling aspects of identity across generations, bringing together what it is to be Eurasian and Queer. Rafeif Ismail contributes her award-winning story of identity, hatred, and the power of love through the ages. And Omar Sakr pens a stark, powerful memoir of connection and disconnection, sharing with us a moment of his life as a Queer Arab-Australian.

Our last group of stories offers perspectives from People of Colour and writers of diverse cultural backgrounds that are grounded in little written-about migrant experiences. Muslim author Amra Pajalic, child of Bosnian migrant parents, writes about struggling to acclimate to monocultural Australian high school life. Wendy Chen shines a light on the lives of Chinese-Australian migrants at the time of Federation. Michelle Aung Thin, Burmese by ethnicity, Canadian, then Australian by circumstance and a migrant many times over, interrogates the process of negotiating who you are in the context of where you are. Alice Pung challenges us to step into the shoes of a teenage boy who comes to question everything he's ever known, or been told, about Asians. Rebecca's contribution rounds out the collection by highlighting what mainstream Australia rarely experiences — what it means to be without privilege, or language, in a new country.

We are the voices too often unheard, the people too often unseen. But we are here; we are speaking. And through this book, we invite you into our worlds.

Meet us at the intersections.

MEET ME at the INTERSECTION

ELLEN VAN NEERVEN

Ellen van Neerven is an Aboriginal writer and poet who comes from the Yugambeh people of South East Queensland. This story is a work of fiction which is grounded in her perspective as a Queer Black woman. Ellen writes, 'growing up in Brisbane, I've always played and been obsessed with football (soccer) and I love our Aboriginal soccer heroes like Kyah Simon, Lydia Williams and Jada Mathyssen-Whyman.'

Night Feet

The scholarship was due today and Dad wasn't home. If I didn't get the scholarship money I wouldn't be going to the Nationals. I tried turning my back to the window and began finishing my application. Every scrape outside could be him.

Dad didn't have a phone. One day he propped his old Nokia up on a ledge above the creek and got my brother and me to take turns throwing rocks at it. We both missed twice and he grew impatient. Knocked it off the cliff himself.

Hours went by too quickly as I lost time cleaning up the kitchen, heating soup on the stove, thinking he'd return for lunch. It was afternoon, and I was still missing a few lines when I remembered we didn't have a printer and I had a game at 8.30 pm.

I filled my backpack, putting in my unwashed strip, shin pads that had been lying outside on the barbecue, and two bottles of water. Importantly, I had a hair tie and a thin band to push back my fringe. I went back and wrote a hurried last sentence on my application. I finished with the words *I love it*, but did I? This had felt like the most important thing in the world once, but last night, today, it had all slipped away. What would happen if I didn't get the money to go to Canberra? I had relied on Dad to be home to work out how we'd get the application in; he would have planned how we'd print it. I would have to work it out for myself.

I'd catch the bus to the library in town, because the post office near it closed later than the local one did. I knew, because Mum used to work there.

There were more people outside the library than in, sitting at the café, standing against the walls talking and hooked into the wi-fi. I hurried through the doors, printed my application and went straight out, with minutes left to post it.

It felt familiar, running to the post office just before closing, across the road, under the bridge, past the pubs starting to get busy and noisy. I didn't like running in my thongs, the V slipping between my toes, but I looked straight ahead and tried to think of an end goal. Like I was on the pitch.

The footpath was blocked off a little farther on, but there was no way I was going to cross the road and back again; I'd lose too much time. I dodged some parked cars and stepped over a patch of water that hadn't drained, and got back on the footpath. Ahead of me, a woman dropped a letter in the express post mailbox outside the post office and I wondered if it was already too late. I half-expected the sliding doors not to open. I ran in and looked frantically around for an envelope. The lady behind the counter said, 'Just a letter? Try an envelope from over there, honey.'

Not just a letter, my inner voice insisted, but I listened to her, and into the kind of happy cream decorative envelope you'd use to send photos of your cat to your grandmother — not the most important document of your life — I folded the application. I scribbled the address from a Post-It and handed the envelope to the lady.

'Just this one?'

'Will it be postmarked today?' I blurted.

'Ah, yeah,' she said. 'I just got to push this back.' I watched her keenly as she picked at the mail stamp, clicking the numbers back. I realised that today was the last day of the month, and that the 28th to the 1st was a big leap. She seemed to struggle with it. Mum could have stood there, where the lady's feet were. She changed the date, stamped my envelope, and I paid her.

I had half an hour until the train to the soccer field and I walked back to the café at the library. I ordered myself a coffee. I'd never had coffee before, but after a sleepless night and with the need for a load of energy tonight, I thought it was a good time to start. I did worry about dehydration, but I had two water bottles, and they could be refilled. With Dad's voice, I said, gruffly, 'Cappuccino, thanks'. I ordered it to go, as they looked like they were packing up. I'd be the machine's last kiss. When they handed it to me, I went and sat in the garden, and watched the people. There was a young black man, African, walking around. I admired his red, new-looking sneakers, a pair like the ones I wanted but Dad would never give me. I could hear the beat of his music, see the yellow buds in his ears. He was wearing a white T-shirt and grey jeans. He looked at me. I sculled the coffee, hot and sudden in my throat. My father's habit. Mum always said to him, *You burn yourself. You'll have no tastebuds left for my casserole.*

The coffee tasted nice, and I already felt less tired. There was a breeze filtering through the garden, caressing my thighs. I chucked the cup in the bin and decided it was time to get changed into my football shorts in the toilets. I stopped for a moment, reopened my bag and took a sip from my water bottle. 'Keep sipping before the game,' Brisbane Roar captain Jade North had said when he came to visit the club. 'Don't gulp.'

I loved North. I rarely had affection for a defender but I loved him because he was a blackfella and a real workhorse. I rested my bag on the slab of concrete on the side of the café. A sitting spot tucked away. This was the corner where I'd had my first kiss, last year, and the feeling of it always returned. I put my bottle down, and the wind picked it up and took it, and it rolled in the direction of the African boy. He caught it easily and handed it back.

'Thanks,' I smiled. 'Crazy wind, hey?'

He nodded. He still had his earphones in but I couldn't hear the music anymore. As I packed my bag up, he took a step closer and said, 'Hey, how you going?'

'Good,' I said. 'And you?'

'Good. Just waiting for friends and that. Where are you from?' he asked.

I half-smiled at the predictability of the question. The easy answer, and what felt true, was to say, 'From here'.

But they always wanted to know more. He didn't buy it, licking his lips.

'My mother's Italian, my father's Aboriginal.'

'Ah,' he said, and repeated it for clarity.

'And where are you from?' I asked. It was only fair.

'I'm from West Africa,' he said, guarded, and of course it was a line from him. What was West Africa?

'What's your name?' he said, looking at me with some sort of understanding.

'Bella. Yours?'

'Akachi,' he mumbled self-consciously.

It took three times to pronounce it properly, but I wanted to. I looked in his eyes.

'I asked because you look different,' he said.

Again, I could have rolled my eyes at the predictability. We looked at each other. I was used to these sorts of moments of connection. Lines of dialogue came in to my head. *Welcome, brother. Thank you, sister.*

'You study, work?'

'I'm still at school,' I said. How old did this fella think I was?

'Oh. Yeah. I study and work.'

'You doing anything interesting tonight?' I asked.

'Waiting for friends. We're going out to the city. I go here to check my emails. You here often?'

'Not really.' I reckoned I should come here more often. 'I've got to get changed,' I said, pointing away.

'Okay,' he said. 'Nice to meet you.' And he made the effort to give me one of the handshakes I'd always wanted, made me feel like one of the boys.

In the bathroom I stood in front of a mirror. I slipped off my singlet and T-shirt bra. My arms were tanned from all those afternoons running in the bush. My small breasts, that I had just noticed a year ago, but my grandmother had obsessed with years before, were pale in comparison. There was a sunburnt strip across my collarbone from the last game. I was still kind of black, though. More so, without clothes. I changed my bra and changed my skirt for shorts. I fixed my hair and looked at my sleepy eyes and said to myself, *Get ready*.

When I got out, Akachi was gone.

At the train station, I used the fifteen minutes to pace, flexing my leg muscles, prepping myself. The station was quiet. I saw some mob with Roar shirts and I was sorry I would miss the game as it would be played at the same time as mine. I thought ahead to my game. An unknown quantity, this opposition. They'd won their first game, narrowly. I wondered if my dad would be there. Was he wondering where I was, whether I'd got my application in and how I'd get to the game? He always took me to the games. I had to ride my bike to training quite a lot, but he always took me to the games.

The lit train crunched into the station, and I felt the studs of my boots dig into my back as I put my backpack back on.

I arrived later than we were meant to and walked the dusty path to the football field. It was lit up and empty, like a runway. The grass looked beautiful. Sparkling. I walked past the group of three refs. I nodded to my coach. Anxious. I hoped he'd play me up front. Most of the girls were already in the dressing room. I touched Casey's shoulder. She was nervous. It was her first game back from being really sick in hospital. I pulled the red-and-black over my head. Completed my pre-game superstitions. Left foot first. Got Casey to tape my right ankle even though it had been a year since the injury. Did my ponytail four times. I watched our lanky goalkeeper, Bronte, eat a banana. She had such an expressive face that, sometimes, when I was nervous, impatient, I would slow down, gather my thoughts, be entertained just by watching her frown at the team sheet.

'We have two subs,' she announced. 'And Bella. You haven't signed.'

I took the sheet from her and scribbled my initials. I had thought my dad would be outside, but he wasn't. Perhaps he was watching the Roar instead, which I didn't mind. He could let me know the score. But perhaps he was still out in the forest in the dark.

We did our usual warm-up. The string of girls flooding past in lines was comforting. How unlike the real game. No randomness. Just repeat, repeat. The ball moving in straight lines. At one point, the passing line broke down, the ball had an uneven delivery, and it bobbled off the ground; the receiver was unable to trap it, and it went over her foot. She raced out to get it, and, with my hands on my hips, I turned and had a look at the opposition. I didn't normally like to do this. It just sets me off. I thought: *Who were the defenders? Any weak links? Does the goalkeeper have anything? Would she dive for my trademark right-hand corner placement?*

My teammates were suddenly squealing; they went soft on me, screaming at the discovery of a toad standing guard on the pitch where the ball had rolled. My coach was on it, running over, and before I could say anything, he kicked the toad with his steel-capped boot. 'Keep going, girls,' he growled.

I was playing on the left wing. My second position. Covering for missing girls. I didn't mind that much. I knew I'd still get my chances. Although I did feel a little self-conscious. I had been chosen to represent State. I was my team's biggest weapon. But I wasn't put where I was most effective. I looked at the two girls playing there, Casey was one of them. She was a defender by birth and always would be. I was angry at the decision. There were no scouts, I didn't have to prove anything, but, at the same time, I did.

During the game, I remembered why I didn't like playing wing. It was a game played in a tunnel. A long, narrow stretch of the park. In defence, I had to tuck in, cover the gap in the middle, and also work with my fullback to cover the space in behind. The transition between defence and attack, and attack and defence, was frustrating. When we got the ball, I'd sprint my guts out, create space for myself wide, but I wouldn't get the ball. A couple of times when I did get it, bunched back in my half, I decided to take on the player, try and use my speed to get around her. But it didn't work. I was too predictable, and got caught; she always had backup.

In defending, I was unenthusiastic. I could feel my goal-scoring energy being sucked up every time I turned on my heel and ran backwards to cover.

We scored early. Donna finished well. I felt relief, and that we would get some more. We had a corner soon after.

During the corner, I stood at the front post, ready to flick anything on. Donna took the corner. The ball went past me and hit an opposing player, a mistimed clearance, and I moved my body so that the ball came to me. I quickly controlled it, got my boot under it, and hit it on the half-volley. Before I knew the outcome of the strike, I thought of my father. Then real time happened and the strike hit the keeper and she saved it. I sprinted backwards, in defence, to swallow it. I suspected then that it would be my best chance of the game.

It was 1—1 at half-time. We weren't happy. Our keeper was trying to pick us up. Casey and I weren't even making jokes like we normally did.

I was better than the girl I was playing. Loads better. But she had her dad egging her on from the sideline. 'Round her!'

I thought my dad would do that if he was there. Except his favourite cheer was 'C'mon!' At one point of the match, she did round me. Conned me, took off, went running into miles of space. I felt foolish and couldn't catch up. I chased her down to the corner flag, but I was nowhere close to making any sort of contact. It didn't cause a goal or anything, but I was annoyed.

I got a message from the coach to swap positions with Casey and jump up front. *Here we go.* I started to get some good touches. Control the match. Put my girls in for some good chances. But on the other end, we copped it. Mistake after mistake, and we were down 3—1. Terrible. I still tried. Whenever Bronte had it in her paws, I took off to make myself an option, got all the high balls.

Lack of sleep was catching up on me. And I was cramping. My calves were stiff.

Towards the end of the game, when both coaches were subbing, and the players were no longer running to get the ball when it went past the sideline, I got the ball in a good position. Casey was behind me, and I gave it to her quickly , hoping to get it back. Yes! She put it through the hole. I was right in on goals. At the keeper again! But the ball bounced off, to Donna, who hit it well. It pushed off the post but I was running so hard at it I didn't see it and there were hands on my shirt and I was on the ground and the ball was in the net. Where did it come off? My knee? Chest? My girls were around me.

I had got my goal, sort of, but it didn't feel any kind of sweet. Before anything else could happen, the ref blew the whistle for the end of the game.

'Where's your dad?' Casey said as we walked barefoot across the field. I realised how drenched in sweat my jersey was.

'I don't know,' I replied.

'We'll take you home,' Casey's mum said.

I clicked the door open cautiously.

'Dad?'

'Bella?'

I felt the emotion that had been building up all day come out as I ran towards Dad, standing against the sink, hair messy and tired-looking, like even too tired for a hug. But I touched his arm, repeating, 'Where were you?'

'I'm sorry, I had to go buy a printer, so I went to Kmart this morning and I just couldn't work out which one to get.'

It sounded like an incomplete excuse as to where he had been all day, but I didn't press him any further.

We sat down at the kitchen table and I slowly rolled my socks off.

'I got so tired, I can't explain it,' Dad said. 'I really miss her, you know, and I end up getting myself in knots because she was your mum. You must miss her so much.'

'You're allowed to miss her, too, Dad.'

He tried to smile. 'How was the game? Did you score?'

'Yeah.' I didn't lift my head.

'I wish I could have seen it.'

'I had to play wing. It was a tough game, Dad. We lost. But we'll get there next time. I caught a train from the city, I passed through and posted—'

'You got the application in,' Dad interrupted, sighing with relief.

'Yeah. We'll be going to Canberra, Dad.' I said it without knowing but feeling, feeling a determination in my feet. My hands brushed over the unpaid bills and the coffee rings stained into the table. 'I printed it at the State Library and I met a nice boy called Akachi who follows Real Madrid.'

Dad looked at me suspiciously.

'What?' I said.

'I thought you liked girls.'

I shrugged. 'It was 3—2. Donna scored the other one.'

'Tell me about your goal.'

'Yeah, I just got my body in the way.'

'Came off your eyebrow?'

'My knee!'

'Good one.'

'Totally intentional,' I said, and my mind started to wander to the next game I'd play, how Dad would be there to see my future goals.

GRAHAM AKHURST

Graham Akhurst is an Aboriginal writer and poet who comes from the Kokomini of Northern Queensland. He lives and works on Yuggerra Country. This poem is informed by the history of colonisation and his own journey towards a culturally strong identity. Graham writes, 'I hope this poem will get people thinking about the powerful intergenerational effects of colonisation, while also seeing the great resilience of Indigenous peoples.'

Dream

Dormant

                                        I see

White walls and circles
                            brown skin

move time
                                contested

and motion

a scratch

rearing
            blood
                    closer
                        to truth

Desert

                                        I witness

Red dust blinds

                                the earth's

concealing
shards

                                     form

that slice

the earth drinks
bloodied footprints

announcing
       the forgotten

Haunted

                                                I watch

The writhing serpent

                                                my place

conjures sparks
        unfolding

                                                in history

Totems struggle

                                        fade

guiding
        balance

Ritual

                                                as sails flex

moves time
I remember everywhen

                                                closer

My blood
        tolerance

In haunted space

KYLE LYNCH

Kyle Lynch lives at the Kurrawang Aboriginal Christian Community in Western Australia. He comes from the Wongi people. This story provides a snapshot of a week in Kyle's life as he looks for a job.

Dear Mate

Day 1, 10.30 am-ish

Dear Mate,
Today I am gunna try and get myself a job. Sick of lazying
around all day.

Walked to my aunty at the KACC office.

Me: Hey, Aunty.

Aunty: Yeah.

Me: I want to get a job.

Aunty: True.

Me: Yeah.

Aunty: That's good.

Me: Well, whattttty.

Aunty: Okay!

Me: You gonna help me or what?

Aunty: Okay.

Me: Well, what I'm gonna do?

Aunty: Well, you need a résumé for starters!

Me: What's that?

Aunty: Mmmm. I'll talk to you tonight.

Me: What. I wanna go now!

Aunty: Where you wanna go?

Me: Town!

Aunty: Just wait for tonight. Me and you talk about it tonight.

Me: Okay!

Now what?
1.26 pm

Day 2, 9.22 am

Dear Mate,
Today I might have a job. Better not forget to ring you know who! Better start early before I waste another day. Never got to talk to Aunty last night.

Walking to the office AGAIN, where Aunty work.

Me: Hey, Aunty.

Aunty: Yeah!

Me: What happen last night? We supposed to talk about job stuff.

Aunty: Yeah. Busy cooking feed all day.

Me: Well!

Aunty: Well, first you need a résumé.

Me: Welllll! What is it?

Aunty: It's something to say, if you worked anywhere else. Your address, and stuff like that.

Me: (thinking hard)

Aunty: What now? You thinking overtime.

Me: Nah. What else?

Aunty: Well, you want me to help you?

Me: Yeah. Or what?

Aunty: What you mean or what!

Me: Nah! Help me!

Aunty: I don't wanna waste my time talking and you're not even gonna listen to me.

Me: Nah! It's right. Let's do this thing.

Aunty: Okay! Well …

Later

Aunty: There you go. It's only one page long, but that's okay.

Me: So what I do with this? Hand it over to the boss person?

Aunty: Yes! You know, manager or someone like a boss.

Me: (smiling at my résumé)

Aunty: That looks good.

Me: Yeah. Looks solid.

Aunty: Let's take some copies.

Me: What for copies? Okay.

Aunty: What you just want to take one in — you need a few to take to different jobs.

Me: I, yeah!

Aunty: Put it in this folder.

Me: Okay. Now what?

Aunty: When you go town, just hand a copy of résumé to whatever job place you want to work.

Me: True.

I go look for a lift to town.

Me: Kanessa, you going town?

Kanessa: After school. I'm waiting for kids to finish school. Why?

Me: I want to go town to drop some résumés off.

Kanessa: Drop some what off?

Me: Résumé.

Kanessa: What you trying to look for a job?

Me: Yeah.

Kanessa: Well, wait after.

Me: Okay. Pick me at Pop's after.

Kanessa: Okay.

Waiting around past 3.30 pm. So I ring my cousin.

Me: Kanessa, where you?

Kanessa: Oh sorry, I'm town. I forgot — I thought you went to town with Pop.

Me: (Hmmm) It's right.

I might as well go home.
3.47 pm

Day 3, 8.10 am

Dear Mate,
Well I got my things together. Better start looking for a lift early.

Walk over to my other cousin's house.

Me: Reuben, take me town.

Reuben: Why?

Me: Are you going town or not?

Reuben: Why?

Me: Because I want to go to town. Derrr.

Reuben: Why you want to go to town?

Me: Because I want to!

Reuben: I gotta go work.

Me: I'll be blowed. Gotta wait all day!

Reuben: Go and find a lift.

Me: Don't worry. You make me sick.

I can't even get a lift. Waiting all day.
    I know, I'll ask Pop if he's going town.

Me: Pop, you going town?

Pop: Yes, in a minute.

Me: Yes, wait for me!

In the car driving to Kalgoorlie with Pop. It's 10.39 am.

Me: Guess what, Pop.

Pop: What?

Me: I'm looking for a job.

Pop: That's good, my boy!

Me: I'm not going to be like those other boys. I'm gonna look for a job.

Pop: Well that's good. I'll be very proud of wherever you work.

Feeling special.

Pop: Where you want me to drop you off?

Me: Main street unna?

Pop: What? Up the main street?

Me: Yeah.

Pop: Okay. Ring me after. I'm going to a meeting.

Me: Okay.

In the main street of Kalgoorlie, Hannan Street. Feeling confused. What now?

Better start looking.

But where first?

Ladah, lots of people everywhere. I'll go for a walk to Macca's first.

In the shop now. What shall I say? Who do I ask for?

I suss the place out. Hope no Wongi here. Ngurnda [Wongutha for shame].

Shall I or shall I not. Okay, here goes.

I'm at the counter facing a lady.

Lady: Can I help you?

Me: Yes … erm … can I have a frozen coke? And who do I talk to to get a job?

Lady: Yes, that will be a dollar and I'll get my supervisor to speak to you.

Me: Okay. Thank you.

Waiting awkwardly at counter.

Supervisor: How may I help you?

Me: Yes, erm, I'm looking for a job.

Supervisor: Take one of these application forms and fill it

out. Bring it back with your résumé.

Pulling résumé out of my pocket. Small as! Folded it a bit too much.

Me: I have this paper here.

I hold out the folded paper to the supervisor, unfolding it.

Supervisor: Bring this back with this application.

Me: Okay. Deuces.

Well, that's over. Better ring pop to pick me up.

Me: Pop, pick me up.

Pop: Where are you?

Me: Macca's near Woollies.

Pop: Okay. Wait there.

Me: Don't take too long!

Trip home with Pop, I showed him the application form, what I needed to complete.
4.30 pm

Day 4, 9.00 am-ish

Dear Mate,
Better get Aunty to help me fill this application out today.

Me: Help me fill this form out?

Aunty: What form?

Me: I got this form from Macca's yesterday.

Aunty: Show me. True as who?

Me: Here then. Look! What's this then?

Aunty: Solid. Let's fill it in.

Me: Okay.

Driving to town with Aunty to hand application in to Macca's.

Aunty: Gone then. Go in and hand it in.

Me: So what I do? Just give these two papers to the lady at the counter?

Aunty: Yeah.

Me: Okay.

'Thug Life' is playing in my head as I walk in to hand over résumé and application.

Ten minutes later

Aunty: What happened?

Me: Nah? I did it.

Aunty: That's good.

Me: Let's go.

Aunty: Well, what they said?

Me: They said I gotta wait for phone call. They going to ring me!

Aunty: Make sure your phone is charged up and can get a signal all the time.

Me: Yeah.

11.32 am

Day 5, 10.00 am

Dear Mate,
I'm just waiting for the phone call. How long, I wonder?

Darryl: Kyle, what you doing? Why are you always looking at your phone? Wanna come motorbike riding with me?

Me: I'm waiting for a phone call from Macca's for a job!

Darryl: What? True?

Me: Nah derr.

Darryl: I want to get a job too!

Me: You can't get a job around here. It's hard.

Darryl: Nah, I'll chop you up.

Me: Is that a joke?

Darryl: Well, what?

Me: When you get older like me you can get a job.

Darryl: When I get older I want to be like you!

Me: Cool.

Feeling all proud and happy
11.32 am

Day 6, 9am

Dear Mate,
Lost my phone last night. LADAH!
    I better start looking for my phone. NOW!
    I have searched everywhere. Where can it be?

12.30 pm, later

Me: Darryl, have you seen my phone? Do you know where I left it last night?

Darryl: I seen your phone last in the lounge room at nana and pop's on charge.

Me: Okay, I'll check.

Darryl: Okay, see ya!

Found it! Sigh.
   Checking for any missed calls from Macca's.
   One missed voicemail!
   Listening to voicemail …

'Hi Kyle, this is the supervisor from Kalgoorlie McDonald's.
   Thank you for your job application. Unfortunately,
   we have received many applications and you were
   unsuccessful for the position. Please try again next time.
   Thank you.'

Me: What!

Oh well. Better luck next time.
1.00 pm

Day 7, 10:30 am

Dear Mate,
Well I waited a couple of days for that phone call. And they didn't even give me the job.

I'm not giving up but feel down about it.

Feeling disappointed by not getting the job ... don't feel like I want to do anything today.

Aunty: What happen?

Me: Nothing ... got the phone call from them Macca's mob.

Aunty: Well ...

Me: Nothing missed out.

Aunty: True ... well, keep trying ... take your résumé to some other places around town.

Me: Yeah ...

Feeling down.

Aunty: Don't forget we gotta go to that workshop tonight.

Me: Argh arg ... I don't want to go tonight.

Aunty: Come along you can catch up with some of your mates there and you will feel much better.

Me: Okay ...

Arrive at workshop at 5.00 pm
Catching up with friends and staff at the workshop!!!

Workshop Coordinator: Tonight we have a guest, she's a staff member from KCGM and she'd like to talk to you about applying for work experience or apprenticeships at the Super Pit gold mine through the equity program they run.

Me: Sound good.

Workshop coordinator: Is anyone here interested in applying for a job at the KCGM? Please come and take an application form.

Hands go up. People hand out forms to us.

Workshop coordinator: Complete the form and bring it back next week to the workshop.

Me: Aunty, shall I go up and get a form … it's for youths between fifteen and seventeen years old.

Aunty: If you're interested … yeah, get one.

Me: Righteo.

Me: Aunty, help me fill this application form out.

Aunty: Let's take it home and bring back next week.

Me: Okay …

7.00 pm

Day 8, 5.00 pm

Dear Mate,
Well we have completed the application form for KCGM last
night. Let's see where this will take me.

The following week at the workshop. Handed in completed
KCGM application form.

KCGM Rep: Thanks, Kyle. I'll get back to you in the next
    couple of weeks to let you know if your application has
    been successful.

Me: Thanks.

Now what?

EZEKIEL KWAYMULLINA

Ezekiel Kwaymullina is an Aboriginal writer who comes from the Palyku people of the Pilbara region of Western Australia. He is dyslexic and couldn't read until he was a teenager. This poem is about his experiences in the classroom as an Aboriginal boy with dyslexia. Ezekiel writes, 'My teachers never noticed that I couldn't read. I just used to sit there, pretending to understand the words.'

Embers

My mind's a fading star
You watched its embers die
Yet you spare no glance
Not even a look
For the boy at the back of the class

OLIVIA MUSCAT

Olivia Muscat, emerging writer and granddaughter of post-World War Two immigrants from Italy and Malta, was born with a severe visual impairment that remained relatively stable until she was thirteen years old, when she developed total blindness. This story is a memoir piece about one of the most pivotal moments of Olivia's life. She writes, 'What I'd most like readers to take away from my story is that people with a disability are not sub-human, or super-human. They, we, are just regular human, with strengths and flaws and embarrassing interests. We may get things done in a slightly different way, which may seem odd to others, but it works for us. It definitely isn't always sunshine and cupcakes, but that's mostly okay, because whose life is? There are other aspects of my life which I consider much more challenging than being blind. I often wonder if and how my life would be different if my blindness had never happened. How different would my adolescence have been? How would it have shaped my adult self differently? Would I have studied the same things? Been on the same career path? Had the same experiences? Viewed myself, my life or other people differently?'

Harry Potter and the Disappearing Pages

Imagine, if you will, a thirteen-year-old girl. Long brown hair, glasses, on the chubby side, most likely wearing a blue and white checked school dress with yellow trim.

Thirteen-year-old Olivia loves 'Harry Potter'. She adores it, cannot imagine a better series. Her favourite character is Nymphadora Tonks and she ships Ron and Hermione so hard that it hurts, and she has done so since she was seven-years-old. Thirteen-year-old Olivia is a romantic. She is also convinced she is a Gryffindor.

This girl is me.

It is 2007 and I have just started year seven at the school that will become my own. It isn't quite mine yet, I'm new and scared and awed and trying to make friends. I've come from my local primary school where I was a very big fish in a very small pond of grade six students. So, the world of blazers and 'twelve little girls in two straight lines' style hats, and fancy science wings and fighting for academic prizes is all new to my overwhelmed brain. I think I'm ready to take it all on.

Life has other plans though.

*

If you too are, or ever were, a 'Harry Potter' fanatic, 2007 was a big year. It was the year that Potter fans across the globe were waiting for. The countdown to July twenty-first was on. My copy of *Deathly Hallows* was pre-ordered, and the theories about hallows and horcruxes and who would die were flowing like butterbeer at the Leaky Cauldron.

In the lead up to this most anticipated July day, strange things started happening to me. No, unfortunately, I couldn't suddenly speak to snakes, and no strange letter from an unknown school arrived to tell me I should purchase a wand and catch the train from platform nine-and-three-quarters. Things did start disappearing though.

Worksheets I used to have no trouble with at school suddenly became almost impossible to read. I started running into things, and people, with somewhat alarming frequency. The people on TV became blurred shapes. My parents asked repeatedly whether I was okay, constantly on the alert because they're my parents. It's what they do. Especially those of a child born with a 'disability'. I had always been visually impaired, but had enough sight to read regular-sized print and get around without a mobility aid. Up until this point, my condition had been relatively stable. I'd tell them *I'm fine. It's nothing. I'm just a bit careless.*

Because that's what I wanted to be true. I was thirteen; I had no view of the long-term consequences. Mum and Dad said they believed me. Looking back now, I'm not sure they ever really did.

The moment that made all of us stop and think maybe the problem was something serious that should be dealt with and not ignored until it hopefully went away, came thanks to our good old friend Harry and his heroic quest to vanquish the Dark Lord. I barely slept at all on the night of the twentieth of July. Perhaps it was anticipation, or perhaps I had some inkling that something wasn't be right, a subconscious knowledge of what would slap me right in the face.

Mum and Dad took me to the bookshop where my pre-ordered copy awaited my greedy hands. The air was heavy with wonder and anticipation. Delighted squeals and squeaks rang out. I was sick with nerves. The book was placed reverently in my hands by the shop assistant and I clutched it feverishly. My mum took a peek at the last page while the shop assistant and I covered our ears, crying out that *We don't want to know anything. Nothing!*

I opened my book as we left the shop and peered hungrily at the pages. I squinted. I strained my eyes to look as hard as I could. I could see black squiggles on the page, but nothing made sense. I couldn't form the black smudges into recognisable shapes, letters and words and felt the worry radiating off my parents. They tried to act casually unconcerned. I snapped the book shut and claimed that the publisher must have changed the font size. *That must be it. It's the only possible explanation.* When we arrived home, I rushed upstairs to grab my copy of *The Order of the Phoenix*, dread growing like a philosopher's stone in my stomach. I held the two books up next to each other and showed my parents. *I'll prove it to you.* By this point I was desperate and they were defeated, but humouring me. I flipped the books open and stared longingly at the pages. There they were again. Those dastardly black smudges. The words that had been so clear to me not one year previously, were now as indecipherable as ancient runes. I dropped the books to the floor and burst into tears.

*

The next few months, and years, were filled with doctors' appointments, specialist consultations, procedures, and quite drastic operations to try and repair the damage. But it was too late. Things just got worse and worse. Everything was tried, to no avail. I was left with no sight. When that fight was lost, a new fight began. The fight that has become the rest of my life. The fight that I continue to fight, and will continue to fight, every day.

The fight to not be ashamed: for being different; for needing to ask for help or special consideration; for sometimes taking longer to do everyday tasks; for not being or feeling the same as I used to; for bursting into tears and having a minor breakdown when I can't get the fucking cupcake mixture into the fucking paper cases without making a fucking mess, and really how hard is that?

The fight to be okay with being different.

The fight to do whatever the hell I want. Whether it's climbing onto a top bunk at school camp, taking a role in a school production or going places alone, I've always had to prove myself. Fight tooth and nail against people who have a lot more authority than me. Beat down the door until the powers that be notice that I'm not an infant, not an invalid, I'm a capable human with wants and aspirations and ambitions, who has every right to explore every avenue open to me and many that are not.

The fight to not be shoved in a box. From the people who expect me to be kind and meek and helpless. To the ones who expect me to be out there inspiring the world. Those who assume my likes and interests, that all my friends are blind, that I am a lover of braille and goal-ball, that I have no interest in fashion, that I don't enjoy movies or television, that I am a super-brain, savant, prodigy, that I lack the mental capacity to string two words together, that I am some sort of goody-two-shoes over achiever, that I have no social life. The list goes on. It is exhausting.

The fight for access. Chasing people up when I still have no textbooks and a course is half over. Emailing customer service at a streaming app three times, because I just want to watch a movie but their new update is totally inaccessible, and never hearing back. Not being able to put on a load of washing because the new machines all have touch screens. Having someone else fill out personal forms for me because in this age of technology they cannot possibly be provided electronically.

The fight to not always be an inspiration, a role model, a poster child. I didn't sign up for this. I didn't choose it. So what makes people think I want any business in promoting the brand? I just want to live my life, have a good time, sometimes do stupid shit, and get on with it, without being scrutinised by a shocked public. I'm here for myself. Not for someone else's idea of what I should be.

The fight to get away from the strangers who feel they have the right to help me, touch me, talk down to me. I am not loving the pity party that the world seems to want to constantly throw me. I have to continually pull away from strangers who grab me and try to direct me, because I obviously can't actually know where I want to be going. Yet, I must be polite about it, lest I offend the stranger who has decided to invade my personal space. I have to constantly speak up when people ask questions about me to whoever I'm with. *Does she want sugar in her coffee? Would she like to pay with cash or card?* I don't know … maybe *she* would like to teach *you* — a lesson about manners.

The fight to never let my frustration show. I constantly bite my tongue, try not to be too harsh, keep some semblance of calm in my tone. When I am forced to argue with somebody about whether I know where I'm off to, reassure a woman who tells me she is going to tie my shoelace that I can manage it myself, confirm for somebody that *I'm working with that*, that I can indeed watch Netflix. There is a constant struggle not to roll my eyes every time somebody tells me I should be patient because some people just don't know better. Has it ever occurred to anybody that this is the part that is most frustrating? That the fact that people don't know better and feel like it is their place to make assumptions about me and my life and what I am capable of is the most agonising part of my existence. That it is up to me to constantly educate the sheltered public is eternally annoying, and not something I take any pleasure in. Maybe I just want to sit on the train and listen to my podcast, fantasise about a boy in my Italian class, brood about life, and not be expected to educate someone on the appropriate etiquette to observe when dealing with a blind person. I do not exist to be a teachable moment. I have better things to do.

The fight for my right to simply exist without being questioned. I am asked how I can use the words *watch, see, look*? People tell me *You don't really think you can have kids do you? Oh*, they say, *You go to university do you? Do you need help? Are you lost? Are you sure you can manage that? Is this person your carer?* All said in a condescending tone that makes me want to rip their eyeballs out and see how they like it. In fact, I do 'look' for my phone when I leave it somewhere stupid. I 'see' my friends on Friday night. I could have kids if I wanted to. And yes I go to university. I finished in the top five per cent of the state in year twelve, actually. But really … none of that stuff is any of your business. If I can't manage something, or I'm lost, I'm capable of asking for help. So, if I'm just casually sitting on the bus, I probably ended up there on purpose. No need for the inquisition. Do you know where *you're* going? I want to scream at them.

The fight to deal with my blindness in the way that works for me. Yes, I have a sense of humour. No, I'm not using jokes as a coping mechanism. I just think jokes are funny. Yes, I am capable and awesome and get on with life. No, it isn't always fine. Some days I want to curl up in a ball and give up, because the society we live in likes to make life stupidly difficult for anyone who is a bit different. Not white? Not straight? Not neurotypical? Not able-bodied? Okay then, let's just make certain you need to work three times as hard to be on an equal footing with the people around you. And when those with the advantages chastise you for trying to put yourself ahead of others by asking that things be made accessible for you, try not to scream at them when you're reassuring them that all you want is equality, a chance to have the same shot as anyone else. It's not nice. But don't worry. It's character building.

If I could go back in time to 2007, and give thirteen-year-old Olivia some advice, I'd tell her not to do anything differently. I might mention that she's a fool for denying that anything is wrong. I might tell her to speak up when she's struggling a bit more, so that maybe people would know what was wrong and teachers would not just assume she's lost her work ethic all of a sudden. I might tell her not to back away from things, not to retreat from life quite so much. But she is me, so even that stage doesn't last for very long. Most of all though, I'd tell her that what she is doing is brave. Keeping on with all the things she loves, being the same sarcastic brat she's always been, it's all good and strong and brave. I'd tell her there will be challenges, endless tests of her patience and positivity, but she has the strength to deal with them and move on. I'd tell her that it's okay to make mistakes, and not to dwell on them when she does. To not bother with people who don't want to bother with her. To not give a crap what anyone thinks, listen to her parents, and not, under any circumstances, to read the 'Harry Potter' play that is released in 2016. It might sound cool to thirteen-year-old Olivia, but it is completely atrocious and she definitely won't like it.

Thirteen-year-old me doesn't really need my advice though. She *is* a Gryffindor. She is a fighter, a joker, a tough girl who can be oversensitive at times. All of her experiences have made me, as an adult dealing with people in the real world, able to keep fighting. Rise up and fight back every time the world tries to force me down or put me in my place. She is awesome, a regular Neville Longbottom — not that she would appreciate that sentiment just yet.

She made me, and I thank her.

MIMI LEE

Mimi Lee, a Chinese-Australian emerging writer and university student who divides her time between Sydney and Shanghai, has written a story that is a blend of fiction and memoir. It seeks to capture the experience of being caught between two countries, in which the lives lived, and identities assumed, are quite separate and distinct. Many of the events in the story are based on real events and deal with her personal experience of living through mental illness for the first time. Mimi writes, 'The darkness of this world rarely makes sense, but there is always hope in love. I am grateful for those who supported me to express myself with God's gift of words. Writing is truly cathartic — it uncovers the words that would've been left unspoken.'

Fragments

It's been five months since the funeral in April, and she's still seeing her psychologist. Fleur Xuan has lost count of how many sessions she's had, but she knows this one is likely to go the same way as the others. She almost feels sorry for her psychologist having to feel sorry for her.

As she walks past the room she had her first session in, she remembers thinking then that an appointment with a psychologist didn't resemble the ones in TV shows. Her psychologist was in the same medical centre as her regular doctor, in a normal room complete with a hospital bed, a desk, three chairs and even a plastic skeleton. No windows, nothing to suggest an effort to cheer up mentally ill people. It was somehow comforting.

Except that she had had to tell her psychologist everything that had happened leading up to that moment. Relive it all again. Stab her heart with the same persistent knife, albeit the blade was now blunter. Or perhaps her skin had grown thicker from the pain.

First session. A clipboard and a pen, ready to record any noteworthy point she recounted. At least that was the same as what she had imagined a psychologist to be like.

Where should she even start?

'Your name is French,' her psychologist commented before Fleur could begin. She was a soft-spoken, gentle-looking Chinese lady who'd also gone to the University of Sydney.

Of course there would be a bilingual psychologist, Fleur thought. *It is Hurstville after all, probably the only suburb other than Chinatown where Chinese shop signs outnumber English ones*. Even with English as her first language, Fleur was comforted that she could use Mandarin to supplement her story. Everything that had contributed to her mental health crash had occurred in China, and all the grief, hurt and betrayal had followed her to Australia despite the physical distance; haunting her memory in a different tongue.

'Yes, my grandma gave me the pet name *Fang Fang* in Chinese before I was even born.' Fleur paused to write down the characters: 芳芳, which her psychologist recognised immediately as the ones used to describe the fragrance of plants.

'My zodiac sign is the ox, and she thought it'd be nice if I had fragrant grass around me so that I wouldn't go hungry.' Fleur let out a small smile at the thought of her grandma. At least she was still alive. Grandma was probably her last real connection to China. 'And Mum carried a bit of the meaning over with a French name. You know I couldn't have the name "Fang Fang" and have everyone in this country pronounce it as *fang*.'

'Yeah, how exhausting if you had to explain that it's pronounced "Fung Fung" every time, and that it doesn't mean the tooth of a venomous snake, right?' her psychologist chuckled, picked up her pen again and settled her clipboard on her leg. Small talk was over.

Words so often lose their colour in the face of mental illness. Words, powerful enough to change the world, break up relationships, tear a family apart, seem too feeble to describe the evils of mental illness. How corrosive, debilitating, isolating it is as it consumes you, while still possessing the power to make you blame yourself for what is happening, or resent others for not understanding.

Yet use words she must.

*

'Dysfunctional families' was not really a term you would ever hear in China. In fact, she wasn't even sure if there was an equivalent term in Chinese. Sure, every family has its own problems, encapsulated in the old saying: '家家有本难念的经'. But simultaneously, the Chinese believed in '家丑不可外扬', the equivalent of *Do not wash your dirty linen in public*. Fang Fang had long ago figured that, collectively, they meant that every family had their own troubles but it was nobody else's business, really.

If you looked at her uncle's side of the family, you would think they were the pride of the entire extended clan — all of the aunties and uncles and cousins and distant kin unrelated by blood would sing their praises constantly, but in truth, envy snarled from the bottom of their hearts.

This uncle seemed to have everything the Chinese could want — money, status, and a 'successful', money-making son to 'continue' the family name. The true Chinese dream.

And what of Fang Fang? The child of an unimpressive daughter who never 'made it' overseas. A failed marriage. A failed career. Fang Fang was doing better than her mother — she'd gotten into a prestigious, world-class university law school. But her achievements could never be that impressive when she was not even born in China. She was the little foreigner. Whenever Fang Fang held a different view, or failed to observe some obscure tradition that seemed obvious to them all, however, her relatives would reprimand her with: *But you are Chinese after all. You can't forget your roots.*

*

Grandpa passed away in April. It would be May by the time they reached China.

The only flight that could carry them from Sydney to Shanghai in time for the funeral was the budget airline that imposed a fourteen-hour transit in a city Fleur had never been to, and did not plan to visit ever again. 04:00 arrival in Kuala Lumpur. 18:00 boarding time to Shanghai. Actual limbo.

Every trip to China before this trip might have been tiring, but at least joy had waited on the other end.

Year after year, instead of spending Christmas and summer back home in Sydney, they would pack suitcases laden with 'authentically Australian' healthcare products for the older relatives and 'original packaged' English-speaking DVDs for the younger ones, and set off for wintery Shanghai. Fleur could never decide if she liked going to Shanghai or not. Part of her insisted: *Of course you do! You love seeing your grandparents!* And that was true. But part of her loathed how draining it was. Financially, yes, but most of all physically and emotionally. Especially emotionally. It was always hard to leave. As her grandparents' age increased, every reunion seemed to herald one less reunion. Any reunion could be the last. How could she have known back in February, telling Grandpa she would be back by the end of the year to see him, that there would be no 'next time'?

Every year, they would approach the only green door in the entire row of apartments. The number '109' was painted in red on the green door, just discernible behind the metal security grill. Fang Fang would press the doorbell on the top left corner, not believing she still had to tiptoe to reach it.

The exhaustion from an eleven-hour flight on top of a two-hour metro ride could never dampen Fang Fang's and her mother's happiness in seeing the two elders. In the first few years, Grandma would open the door without a moment's delay, as if she had been counting down the hours, the minutes, the seconds, until the doorbell rang. After Grandma took up residence in a rehabilitation hospital, Grandpa would shuffle up to the door after a while, and after asking them if they had a good flight, would clasp Fang Fang's hands in his and say, 'I've just been re-reading your old letters!'

No more joy from Grandpa waiting for her in China. No more letter writing. No more airmail from '5/57 Oxford St Hurstville NSW 2220 Australia' to '中国上海市普陀区曹杨七村 299 号 109 室 (Shanghai, PRC)'.

No more Grandpa, on this earth.

The tears threatened to burst out like hot water from a boiled kettle again. Fleur quickly rubbed her eyes, and put the metaphysical lid back on before she could erupt.

She needed to do something. Anything to distract herself.

She dug out a pen and the flight confirmation papers, and set her pen off on the blank spaces between the printed words:

> *I don't know how we're going to face the funeral.*
> *Part of me just wants to cry and shut everyone*

out. Part of me knows basic courtesy is still required around relatives, regardless of whether they truly cared for grandpa in their hearts or not.

I want to support Mum, & I'm sure she wants to support me too. We're just both not in the state to do that well.

Why did Uncle lie to us? Why make out as if Grandpa's illness was 'nothing serious' — push us up to the hill of hope before plunging us into the abyss with the sudden news of his death? Why insist that Mum shouldn't go back to take care of grandpa and then blow the smoke of guilt in our faces when it was all too late, saying we did nothing to help?

If Grandpa's condition really was so bad, near the end — why prevent us from seeing him one last time? Why didn't Uncle send him to a hospital to receive proper treatment at the earliest time? It wasn't as if Uncle couldn't afford it! It wasn't as if they lived in a remote country town with no access to medical help! It was 大上海! Big city Shanghai, for heaven's sake.

The more Mum and I think about it, the more suspicious Uncle's conduct becomes. As if he was hiding something from us. Taking advantage of the fact that we live all the way over in Australia

*so that he can mask the truth or twist it however
he wants, knowing full well that he's been our
only channel of information regarding Grandpa's
health condition.*

*When he didn't reply for days on end,
ignoring every frantic phone call and Wechat
message sent by Mum, we knew something was
off.*

*When Mum's old uni friends told her he was
in a nursing home instead of a proper hospital,
& that the carers strongly advised Uncle to
take Grandpa to proper doctors for his bleeding
situation, Mum lost it.*

*What kind of a son says 'I'll think about it' in
terms of saving his own father's life?!*

*'He did it on purpose. He didn't want him to
live,' said a relative who may be the only relative
who cared about Grandpa as much as we did.*

*We cannot even conceive of that possibility.
He wouldn't. Couldn't.*

*

Fleur remembered how, at that first session, her psychologist
had widened her eyes in the same incredulous expression
she'd seen on the faces of her Sydney friends when she had

finally opened up to them in July.

'Had there been any family conflict that might have led your uncle to be so …'

'Callous?' Fleur finished for her.

None that she nor her Mum had created. If anything, they'd both tried to stay out of any conflict. Always taking a step back, always offering reconciliation. But any act of kindness was taken as weakness, acquiescence for the uncle to climb one step higher upon their heads.

Fleur told her psychologist about being in the kitchen, helping her aunt to prepare Chinese New Year's Eve dinner, when it had happened. Grandpa's apartment was not large — the front door opened into the kitchen. A tiny corridor on the right-hand side of the stove led into the living room, which doubled as the dining room. Grandpa positioned his desk under the window, creating an impromptu office space.

As tradition demanded Uncle's presence as a son, Chinese New Year's Eve was one of the only times Uncle ever deigned to visit Grandpa. To bring Grandpa's attention to his arrival, he would put his meaty hand on Grandpa's shoulder — regardless of whether grandpa was engrossed in a history book or the stock market trends — and offer some kind of grunt as hello.

Grandpa would look up, peer at him from behind his heavy glasses that magnified his eyes, and say, 'Oh, you're here.'

In response, there would be no *How has your health*

been, Dad? Have you been sleeping well? Eating well? Classic questions of care that demonstrated filial piety, questions that Fang Fang's mother would ask without fail, and not because she was obligated by tradition to do so.

At the demand of the aunt for more pak choy, Fang Fang's mother left to pick up more groceries for the family feast. Fang Fang was left to have a strained conversation with her aunt, who refused to believe that Fang Fang and her mother could resist all of the shopping centres, restaurants and tourist attractions in Shanghai to stay in this dingy unit with Grandpa.

'Grandpa and I chat.'

A scoff. 'You'll need to shout for him to hear you.'

'But he can read. We communicate with pens. Written words.'

Fang Fang discerned a slight pause in her aunt's stir-frying action. She hoped the pause was from a twinge of guilt.

'No! Absolutely not!' her uncle bellowed in the other room.

Fang Fang sprang back in shock. Her aunt turned off the stove halfway through her braised pork dish and peered down the corridor with her.

Her uncle was standing next to Grandpa's desk, his left fist clenched tight. His facial features intensified, scrunched together in the centre of his face. He was nearly six-foot, complete with a potbelly and unnaturally black hair combed back to hide his balding spot. The classic look of a Chinese official pampered with too many under-the-table treats at fatty feasts.

A low growl from Uncle ensued: 'This apartment is *mine*. It's been under my name since it was bought. I will never agree to dividing its value with her!'

'Her' undoubtedly referred to Fang Fang's mother, who told Grandpa from the outset that this wasn't a good idea, that her brother's love for money would turn her into his enemy.

But what her uncle deliberately left out — or perhaps had long forgotten — was that this apartment had been bought by Grandpa with his own money. Back when Uncle and his wife were struggling as laid-off workers, Grandpa had bought two apartments and put them both in his son's name to provide him with some sense of security. At that time, Fang Fang's mother had still been married, living in a two-storey house in a northern Sydney suburb. She'd had no problem with her father's decision to help out her brother in this way.

Now, Fang Fang's mother was the one who was struggling as a single mother. Fang Fang was the only child in the extended family who was still studying. Surely it was not unreasonable to want to leave something for them? Grandpa must have said this, or uncle would not have flown into a rage in this way.

Her aunt's face was turning more scarlet by the minute.

Not from shame, but from anger. Self-righteous anger.

'You're going to take what rightfully belongs to me, *me*, your only son, for *her*? Someone who's not even a citizen of our country?' her uncle raised his voice even louder. 'You're not going to give her any of my money. I'll never agree to this!'

Grandpa raised his voice too. 'This is my decision and my money to divide. You are both my children no matter where you live. Are you signing the agreement or not?'

For someone who didn't grow up with a father, the sight of two men arguing froze Fang Fang in place.

Her uncle scrunched up the piece of paper Grandpa was holding out to him and stormed towards the kitchen. Fang Fang didn't move, couldn't move — the potato she had been peeling was still in her hand. She should move to make room for him to pass through, but what if her movement reminded her uncle of her existence, prompting him to attack?

Uncle shoved past her roughly. The man who had been so used to being right, so used to being lifted up in the sky by family praises and compliments, looked like a four-year-old deprived of his favourite toy. Except that his face burned more viciously than a childish tantrum, his eyes glowered more hatefully than could be expected from a family member. He tilted his head at the front door, and his wife, whose face resembled melting red wax, turned resolutely and walked out before him. Fang Fang could not believe they were walking out of a New Year's Eve dinner.

It had been the first major rift in the relationship.

Money 1; family 0.

*

'He let him die because of money. You should've seen him as soon as the funeral ended — he was all smiles. As if he'd just rid himself of a burden,' Fleur told her psychologist.

'I guess he has the money all to himself now,' the psychologist mused.

'But he's still not satisfied. Mum never wanted to fight with him over money precisely because he was her brother. We've done nothing wrong, but he has never stopped attacking and antagonising us since that argument with Grandpa. He even had the audacity to tell us he refused Grandpa's dying wish of leaving us some money. *I stopped him* was what Uncle said. As if he had done a glorious thing, refusing a dying man's wish — his own father's dying wish. Absolutely no remorse. I never realised such … evil, could exist in my own family. At least we always saw him as family. But now I realise he sees us as outsiders — ever since Mum moved away.'

Organ failure, resulting from intentional negligence, resulting in the victim bleeding to death, slowly and painfully. Grandpa had died without dignity. Without love.

Without true family beside him. Fleur would've never found out the truth if her mother hadn't called up the carers in the nursing home herself.

How was one supposed to feel when the victim of this crime of neglect was none other than *her* dear grandfather, who'd taught her Tang poetry, chastised her with classical idioms, discussed world politics with her, shared buckets of snacks with her … the one person who'd left an indelible mark on her by training her in Chinese handwriting. His style of calligraphy was so evident in hers that her HSC Chinese teacher had noted that Fleur's handwriting had a male quality to it.

Until the world came crashing down in June, Fleur had never imagined she was capable of feeling so down for so long. Even smiling was an effort, and even when it came, the expression felt so alien to her facial muscles that she always checked herself. Even talking could trigger a flood of tears. Even singing to Disney songs could not lift her mood. She hadn't believed she could deteriorate like this.

Ever since the funeral, she'd been like an overfilled, boiling kettle; ignored for too long on high heat. But the lid put on grief was never meant to hold forever and much like that kettle, would eventually spurt out burning water.

She had not been stronger than her mother, nor was she indifferent or recovering. She had been distracting herself with university, an internship, friends, bushwalks, social events, social media … hoping the passage of time would cure her pain. All the while, her internal wounds boiled and boiled. The lid she had put on her grief was only effective for so long. It had allowed her to function for a time — to smile, to respond to this society that still went on as if nothing had happened, as if nobody had been lost.

Adjustment disorder, her regular doctor had written on her special consideration application form. The term sounded almost benign compared to the *extremely severe depressive and anxiety symptoms* her psychologist said she was experiencing.

*

Only ten minutes until her fifth psychology session. As she sits in the waiting room, she anticipates the usual *How are you feeling?* question, and feels for her psychologist (and for herself), when she anticipates the answer will be: *My grandma passed away last Thursday.*

Five months after Grandpa.

Back to square one in the grief stakes.

A double blow. Two deaths in one year.

She imagines the smile that will follow her words. The sad kind, the *I'm-trying-to-look-better-than-I-am* smile, the *I-don't-know-how-to-cope* grimace, the *people-think-I-should-be-crying-but-my-tears-are-all-dried-up* chuckle.

But, somehow, she knows it'll be easier to cope this time. The deepest cracks in her heart are slowly perfused by the love her mother and friends have shown her, ensuring her that even the most insidious of scars will heal. She's never realised how powerful and liberating the simple act of opening up her heart and talking to someone about her struggles could be — how her burdens could be lessened by the presence of a listening ear. Every prayer, every word of comfort, every moment spent together, reminds her of the greater love, the greater vision and preciousness of life.

Mental illness is just as every other illness — if a cold needs time to heal, why did she expect herself to be exempt from the same process?

Ads for cheap flights to Shanghai flash up on her Facebook newsfeed as she looks down at it in the waiting room.

It's September. She imagines she won't be missing another Australian summer for the coldness of China for a very long time to come.

JESSICA WALTON

Jessica Walton, Melbourne-based emerging author and disability advocate, is a cisgender, bisexual/queer, disabled, white woman with Irish heritage. Her disability is physical, stemming from childhood cancer (osteosarcoma) that resulted in the amputation of her left leg above the knee. She lives with anxiety and chronic pain, including phantom pain — the sensation that her amputated limb is still there. Jessica writes, 'As a queer, disabled teenager I never had stories about people like me. When I was eighteen, my girlfriend (now wife) introduced me to websites where queer people were writing themselves into stories. Reading them was a powerful experience for me, but it still meant something the first time I read a queer character in a published book. I didn't find a book with a queer amputee character until I was in my thirties. 'Stars In Our Eyes' is the kind of story I would have liked to read as a teenager. I want to live in a world where LGBTIQA+ and disabled characters are as common on the page as they are in the real world.'

Stars in Our Eyes

'So who would you kiss: Rey, Rose, Finn or Po?'

I sighed. Mum kept forgetting that daydreaming about being *Star Wars* characters and making out with other *Star Wars* characters was *her* hobby, not mine. She has always been Star Wars obsessed. One of my earliest memories was unwrapping a Christmas present I'd hoped was a teddy bear. Mum still had a photo of me in the tiny Chewbacca costume she'd given me instead.

'God, Mum. They're all *way* too old for me. But you know Rey is aromantic asexual, so let's at least take her off the list.'

'But Reylo!'

'No. For the last time Mum, no.'

'Who then?'

'Easy. Barb from *Stranger Things*.'

'Oh, Maisie, I can see it right now. My daughter, saving poor Barb from the Demogorgon.'

'Or Stevonnie!'

'From *Steven Universe*? Oh, excellent choice!'

'You know most parents don't watch *Steven Universe*, right?'

'I'm trying to stay hip.'

'Who are *you* snogging, then?'

Mum took one hand off the steering wheel to press it to her heart. 'You know who I love!'

'I can't believe you want to kiss Han Solo.'

'I can't believe there's anyone alive who *doesn't* want to kiss Han Solo,' Mum laughed. 'Say you love me, Maisie.'

Mum's way of saying, *remember*. Remember you have me and I have you, no matter what.

'I love you.'

'I know!'

She was laughing again as we pulled into the carpark of the hotel where the Stars in Our Eyes convention was being held. I opened my window and stuck my head out as we neared the disabled bays.

'They're all full, Mum! Don't worry, just park wherever and I'll do the walk.'

'Let's wait a minute. I have a feeling.'

'There is no *way* anyone is leaving these parking spots this close to the start time.'

But as soon as the words left my mouth, one of the cars began backing out.

'*There's no WAY anyone is leaving these parking spots,*' said Mum in her sarcastic fake-Maisie voice as she pulled into the bay and turned off the engine.

'How'd you know?'

'I am one with the Force and the Force is with me.'

She eyed me hopefully. I gave her the Yoda imitation I knew she was looking for. 'The Force is strong with this one.'

I opened my door, twisting my body around so I could swing my prosthetic leg out. I could feel a painful buzzing sensation starting deep in my lower back. If I didn't do something about it soon it'd turn into a razor-sharp spasm shooting from my back down into my stump, and then beyond it, into my phantom limb, which had been gone for almost five years. I patted my pocket to make sure my painkillers were there. I just needed to find food first, so they didn't make me sick.

Mum was at my side. 'I heard they've got food stalls inside.' She'd noticed me touching my pocket. 'We should have time to get something before the first panel.'

Her voice was too cheerful, the way it got when she didn't want me to know she was worrying about me. It was how I always knew when she was worrying.

'I'm okay, Mum.'

'I know that! I just …' She stopped, shaking her head like she could shake off the worry.

'Really, I'm fine.'

We walked in silence for a while, then Mum said, 'So, are you getting Kara Bufano to sign your *Midnight Girls* book today?'

Her voice was still too cheerful, but not as bad. I rolled

my eyes. 'You don't get actors from a film adaptation to sign the original book, Mum! You only get the author to sign the book. How are you so clueless? I'll get Kara to sign my convention t-shirt, once I have one.'

'Rightio,' said Mum. 'I don't get the appeal of signatures. I'd rather have a memorable *moment* with someone I admire. You know, something meaningful.'

'Hey! I want a memorable, meaningful moment with them too, but I want it captured in an epic Instagram selfie while wearing or holding up a limited-edition thingamabob with their signature on it!'

'You're weird.'

'You're weirder.'

We'd reached the volunteers taking tickets. I ended up in front of a tall, lanky teenager with long black hair, freckles, and green eyes. At least, they were mostly green. There were flecks of brown and gold in them too.

'Hi, um, do you have a ticket?'

I'd been staring. My cheeks heated up. I handed the tickets over, avoiding looking at those extraordinary eyes. That was when I noticed the t-shirt — black and covered in glitter with the words NON-BINARY STAR SYSTEM in shimmery silver across the front.

'Nice t-shirt!'

'Thanks. I like puns. Oh hey, I love your t-shirt, too!'

That would be the t-shirt that said 'IT'S RUDE TO STARE'. *Great, Maisie. You stared while wearing a t-shirt telling people off for staring.*

I hurried to explain. 'I get sick of people looking at me when I'm limping, or when they realise I have a prosthetic leg.'

'I get it. I'm sick of people assuming they know my gender and pronouns.'

'What *are* your pronouns?'

'They/them. What about you?'

'She/her. Also, I'm Maisie.'

'Nice to meet you. I'm Ollie.'

I looked up into their eyes again. My tummy did a somersault.

Not now, tummy. Get it together.

'So, um, thanks for taking our tickets.' *Smooth, Maisie. Real smooth.*

'It's nothing. It's my job,' said Ollie. 'Not that I'm getting paid. I mean, I'm getting free entry, so I guess that's … anyway, it's fine.'

There was a quiet chuckle behind me. Mum reached across to shake their hand.

'Hi Ollie! I'm Maisie's mum. You're a bit young to be doing door duties alone, aren't you?'

'Mum, be cool,' I muttered.

'I'm fifteen,' Ollie replied. 'That's old enough to be a volunteer here, if I'm with my dad. He just ducked inside to grab us drinks.'

Mum beamed at me. 'We should volunteer when you

turn fifteen next year!' She turned the smile on Ollie. 'Do you have any panel recommendations?'

'*Fantasy Queers* is the one I'm hanging out for.'

'Me, too!' I said.

'Maisie's been talking about that panel for weeks.' Mum ruffled my hair and added proudly, 'She just came out to me as bi a few weeks ago.'

I gasped. 'Holy shit, Mum, I told you to be cool!'

'Hey, I'm bi too,' said Ollie. 'Welcome to the dark side.'

Mum opened her mouth, no doubt to say something even more embarrassing. I dragged her away, throwing Ollie an apologetic glance as we went. They smiled. It made their eyes sparkle.

Mum nudged me. 'Ollie *likes* you!'

I glared at her. 'Mum, you outed me to a stranger! You know that's not okay, right?'

Mum's shoulders slumped. 'But … I could tell you liked them! And … and … thanks to me we've established that you're both bi, and you're both going to *Fantasy Queers*.'

She'd really thought she was helping, and she sort of had, even if it had been in an awkward, super-embarrassing, boundary-disrespecting kind of way. I couldn't keep up the glare.

Mum brightened as I stopped frowning, and added, 'Plus, most importantly, they've already met their future mother-in-law, and she approves.'

'Oh my god, Mum. I love you, but … *try* and be cool if

we run into Ollie again.'

I took a step forward, and stopped. The hotel lobby was big. The rooms beyond it were big. There were rows and rows of stalls and people everywhere, talking and jostling and buying things. Some were in awesome costumes. I loved the costumes, but there were too many people.

Mum squeezed my arm. 'Don't worry, kiddo. You'll get used to it.'

I wouldn't. I never did. But I knew how to manage it. I focused on my breathing, getting it nice and slow and steady, then I looked at my shoelaces. I counted each of the eyelets and took note of the way each lace passed through each hole. Finally, my anxiety passed. No one was staring at me right now, even though it felt like it. They weren't hostile. They were just a bunch of people in the same place at the same time. Some of them might even be feeling as exposed and alone as I did in crowds. I let the noise of the people wash over me and took a deep breath. 'I am one with the Force, and the Force is with me.'

'That's my girl,' Mum said. 'Let's go find some food.'

*

We settled into our seats, waiting for *Predicting the Future: Dystopia or Utopia* to start. I hated the chairs they used at events like this. My prosthetic foot didn't reach the floor, meaning my leg was just kind of hanging from my body as

I sat. Even with the painkillers I'd taken earlier, I knew my back would get really sore if I didn't do something. I grabbed my backpack from under the seat and positioned it beneath my feet.

Next to *Fantasy Queers*, this was the panel I'd been looking forward to most. I couldn't quite believe I was about to see Kara Bufano, Luna herself, in the flesh. *An amputee. Like me.* I loved the way Luna valued her vulnerability and sensitivity, defending them as strengths she brought to a team full of hardened, kick-arse warriors. Nightshade might be the main character, but Luna was the heart of the *Midnight Girls*.

I was lost in a daydream of myself as Luna when a sweaty, nervous volunteer ruined the moment. 'I'm sorry everyone,' he said into the mic. 'Kara Bufano is feeling unwell and can't make it to the panel. She's being treated by our very qualified first aid team—'

He kept talking but I didn't hear anything else. Kara wasn't coming. Tears welled up in my eyes. I wanted to get up, walk to the car, and go home.

I knew I was being ridiculous. It was one panel. One person.

One person who was an amputee like me. One person who made me feel like maybe I could be a superhero, too.

'I'm so sorry sweetheart.' Mum said. 'But they said she's being treated — maybe there'll be a chance to see her later.'

I nodded. I couldn't push words past the lump in my throat. A tear slid down my cheek. *I've got to pull myself together.* I focused on the *Fantasy Queers* panel. Would there be many other teens in the audience? Would they be queer teens? It wasn't the same as seeing Luna. But it was still something. It was still a chance to meet people like me. I loved my town, but it's not like there were pride parades or queer social events back home.

Mum suddenly started waving enthusiastically. 'OLLIE! OVER HERE!'

I wiped at my cheeks as Ollie and their dad came over. Ollie sat next to me, and their dad sat next to them. The two of us were bookended by parentals. Not an ideal second-conversation-with-your-new-crush situation.

'Hello again, Ollie!' Mum said, bending forward to see past me. 'And hello Ollie's dad. I'm Jo.'

'That's weird, so am I,' he said.

'You're Jo, too?'

'Joe two, even.' Ollie's dad held up two of his fingers. 'Get it?'

Ollie looked as embarrassed as I was sure I had earlier.

'Oh my god, Dad.'

Ollie's dad grinned at them, then said to Mum, 'I might come and sit next to you so these kids can catch up.'

I heaved a sigh of relief as he moved over to Mum and the two of them starting chatting. Ollie and I had as much privacy as we were going to get with my mum and their dad right next to us.

I tried to think of something to say to Ollie. Nothing seemed cool enough.

Then they spoke, 'Are you okay?'

'Yeah, I'm fine. Just … Kara Bufano is sick, so she's not doing any panels. She's kind of why we came to *Stars In Our Eyes* in the first place.'

'That sucks. *Midnight Girls* is awesome. Everyone's always telling me to read the book.'

'It's *so* good! I'll show you my copy. The illustrations are epic.'

'So you're a massive, proper *Midnight Girls* fan? I'm here for *Twisted Beasts*.'

'Oh, I love that show! *RELEASE THE KRAKEN!*'

'It's the first time I've *ever* seen myself in anything.' Ollie said. 'Asterion is me, basically.'

'Except for the bull head.'

'I only put that on occasionally.'

'*Midnight Girls* was that show for me.' I told them. 'First time seeing an actual amputee playing an amputee on screen.'

'Shame her character's not bi, too.'

'She is in my head.'

'I hear you.'

There was a sudden burst of laughter to my right.

'Bloody hell, Dad,' Ollie muttered. 'Ease up on the braying.'

'Don't worry,' I said. 'My mum laughs like a drunken chipmunk.'

'What do you sound like when you laugh?'

'Guess you'll have to say something funny if you want to know.'

Ollie smiled a smile that lit up the gold in their eyes. 'I'll work on that.'

*

We lounged on the couches, just Ollie and me. Their dad and my mum had taken the hint and left us alone. Ollie had been reading my copy of *Midnight Girls*. I'd been drawing in my sketchbook. I didn't know how long the parentals had been gone. It seemed like Ollie and me were in a bubble of time all our own that stretched on forever. Only it didn't. Ollie was from a small town like me, but their town was a long way from mine. We didn't have forever. We only had today.

I took out the drawing I'd been working on and handed it to them. 'Here. Present for you.'

Ollie stared down at the page. 'Maisie, wow. This is amazing!'

They really like it! I hope they get it. They can't not get it, Luna's blowing Asterion a kiss!

Ollie didn't say anything else. Just sat there, looking at the page. *Oh no, I wonder if it was too much? What if they don't like me like that?* 'I'm sorry — I didn't mean to make you uncomfortable ...'

Ollie shook their head. 'It isn't that. No one back home really gets me, or likes the shows and books I like, and ... yeah. Sorry. This is just so awesome. Asterion actually *looks* like me here.' Their mouth twisted. 'Guess we can be whoever we want, in pictures.'

'Maybe we can be in real life too. Our own kind of superhero, at least ...'

'Yeah. Maybe.'

They didn't sound convinced. 'Hey, I'm an awkward hugger, but you could use a hug right now, yeah?'

Ollie stood up and I did too. I prepared myself for the usual uncomfortable balance fail, but instead found myself snuggling into their chest with Ollie resting their chin rest gently on the top of my head. We were two people, leaning in and holding each other up, and it didn't feel awkward at all.

It felt like what life should be like.

*

I walked toward *Fantasy Queers* with Ollie's hand in mine, feeling giddy and happy. Once I was settled in my seat, backpack under my feet, I pulled out my phone.

> We're here, Mum. Front row, in the middle. You on your way?

UM. NO. I MAY HAVE FALLEN OVER
A FOLD OUT CHAIR. I DON'T THINK
I'LL MAKE THIS PANEL. OLLIE'S DAD
IS ON HIS WAY TO CHECK ON BOTH
OF YOU.

Mum! Are you OK?!?

I'M FINE. JUST NEEDED A BANDAID
OR TWO ON MY KNEE. IT'S BANGED
UP BUT I DON'T THINK THEY'LL
HAVE TO AMPUTATE. THERE'S A NICE
FIRST AIDER HERE FUSSING OVER
ME. I EVEN GOT A CUP OF TEA.

Let me know if you need me, Mum.
I'm a bit worried.

I'M WORRIED TOO. WANT TO
MAKE SURE YOU AND OLLIE AREN'T
JOINED AT THE TONSILS YET. IF YOU
ARE, THE FIRST AIDERS MAY HAVE
SOME KIND OF TREATMENT FOR
THAT. LET ME KNOW.

Gross, Mum. We were just talking.

LIKELY STORY.

I'm putting my phone away, you
weirdo.

'My mum fell over a chair, she's in first aid, she's fine, and
your dad's on his way.'

'What?!' said Ollie. 'Better not let him see us holding
hands, or we'll never hear the end of it.'

'Oh believe me, they think we're doing more than holding hands.'

'Reeeally?' said Ollie. 'Well, I'd hate to disappoint them.'

For a moment it was perfect. We kissed once, gently. Then again, a little more confidently.

'Jesus Christ,' said Joe, and my whole body jumped with the shock of being caught mid-kiss.

'Your mum was right, you kids *are* making out!' he said. 'Damn it, now I owe her ten dollars.'

My chair started to wobble as I tried shifting back into my seat, away from Ollie. Suddenly, it collapsed.

Ollie offered me a hand. 'Are you all right?'

'I'm fine. Bloody flimsy chairs. I guess chair-related injuries are a family affair today.'

Joe picked up my chair and put it back into place, and I carefully sat down again.

My first kiss had ended a little dramatically, but it was still amazing. Here I was, a few weeks after coming out, about to watch a queer panel after kissing someone I *really* liked.

I turned around to look at the people behind me. Twisting hurt my back, but it was worth it to see what a *Fantasy Queers* audience looked like. I was pleasantly surprised. Since coming out I'd wondered if I should get a new haircut or update my wardrobe, but the people around me looked all kinds of ways. I felt like I belonged here, just as I was.

Maybe next time I felt lonely or isolated back home, I'd

pull that feeling out and remind myself that there were lots of people like me out there, and I could find them again when I needed to.

*

I got out my phone and looked at the selfies I'd taken with Ollie before we said our goodbyes. I had somehow convinced a bunch of nearby cosplaying Thors to stand in the background, and Ollie and I had these massive, goofy, happy smiles on our faces. My heart hurt. My leg, too.

Mum spoke from the driver's seat, 'Hey, take your leg off, kiddo. You're not going to need it for the next few hours.'

I released the valve on my prosthesis and pulled my stump out of the socket. Even with a liner on, the socket had broken my skin in a few places. I dropped my leg onto the back seat and turned my attention to the silicone liner. I peeled it off, taking a deep breath as the air hit my stump.

Finally.

My leg felt better. My heart didn't.

'Mum, Ollie lives so far away. I know we've only known each other for one day, but … it's *real*. How are we going to do a long-distance relationship? I've never even *had* a relationship. I'm only fourteen!'

'And they're only fifteen,' Mum said. 'I do understand, Maisie. You two had an instant connection. Sometimes these things last for a day, and sometimes they last longer. If it *was* a one-day thing, it doesn't make it any less special or meaningful. Just take it a day at a time from here though, all right kiddo? You have so much time to work out who you are, and what you want to do, and who you want to be with. Take it from me, you don't want to rush into anything. Have fun being fourteen. It goes so fast.'

'This really sucks, Mum. I miss them already.'

'Take a look in my bag,' Mum said. 'I was going to save the surprise for tonight, but I think you need it now. There's a t-shirt in there somewhere.'

I finally found it and held it up.

'Oh my god, Mum. Oh my god. No *way!* How did you get a *Midnight Girls* t-shirt signed by Kara Bufano?'

'Your embarrassing old mum met her in sick bay, just for a minute or two. I told her about how much you admire her, so she offered to sign something for you. She said to tell you she's sorry she couldn't make the panel, but she'd been puking all morning.'

I couldn't believe it. I just sat there, staring at the t-shirt and imagining Kara signing it. Now I could wear it everywhere and remember how special today had been: Ollie, my first kiss, the Queer Panel, and a t-shirt signed by Kara Bufano.

'This will get me a *tonne* of likes on Instagram. Thanks, Mum.'

'Just remember to tell them your mum fell over a chair

and risked getting puked on to get it,' said Mum, laughing as she started the engine.

'I love you, Mum.'

'I know.'

KELLY GARDINER

Kelly Gardiner is a queer writer, editor and educator, who lives and works across Australia and New Zealand. 'Trouble' is historical fiction, but based on something that happened to her one night on St Kilda pier when she was a teenager. Set in an era when queer people were becoming visible in Australia, if only to each other, 'Trouble' portrays a time (1950s Melbourne) when working-class lesbians could find each other in nightclubs, cafés and bars — moments that were sometimes secret yet hidden in plain sight. Kelly writes, 'I grew up queer in a world where it was forbidden. Girls like me knew nothing of lesbian subcultures. There were very few cultural representations of our lives — no films or TV shows with queer characters (except a few murderers!), no books like this anthology, no internet. We were isolated but, eventually, through accident or perseverance, we found other people like us, and found ourselves. I wanted to write a story that isn't about shame, and secrets, and coming out, but about hope and resistance and — perhaps — the first glimmers of love.'

Trouble

Melbourne
Summer, 1957

Someone's shouting at me.

'Hey, *bella*! Where'd you steal the wheels?'

I pretend I can't hear over the engines, and keep my eyes on the traffic lights.

Please turn green. *Please*.

But there's something about the voice. I glance left and there you are.

Leather jacket. Jeans. Short hair. A woman.

You wink and roar away. The light's still red.

*

'I swear, if James Dean was a woman and lived in Australia, that's what she'd look like.'

'That's a big *if*,' says Dot. 'That's a lot of big ifs.'

'Also,' I say, 'if she was Italian.'

Dot hangs the spanner on a nail, wipes her hands on an oily rag — as if that's going to help — and rests one hip against the workbench. Now she's finished doing complicated things to my scooter, she settles in for a chat.

'Let me get this straight. You saw someone who looks like Annette Funicello but dresses like Jimmy Dean? You sure you were awake when this pop singer with movie star looks appeared?'

'I know it sounds far-fetched.'

'And she was riding along St Kilda Road, yeah? Was Mickey Mouse there too?'

'Very funny.'

'And what did she say to you?' Dot swings herself up on to the bench, boots dangling, evil grin. 'Did she challenge you to a race?'

'You've seen *Rebel Without a Cause* too many times,' I say. 'Actually, she laughed at my scooter.'

'Fair enough, too. Jimmy Dean's got taste. What was she riding?'

'A silver Triumph.'

'Nice. And you on the bright orange Vespa. That would be pretty funny.'

'It's the height of style, thank you very much.'

'Rubbish,' she says. 'You look like my Nana, pottering along.' She scratches her nose, leaving a black smudge like a moustache. I decide not to tell her.

'I look like Audrey Hepburn in *Roman Holiday*.'

'Who told you that, Nance?'

'Ask anyone.' Sure, my hair is longer, and my legs are shorter, but I try to look like Miss Hepburn at all times.

'Will I ask Jimmy Dean?'

'So you *do* know her.' Of course she does. Dot's garage is like a magnet for every girl in town with a motorbike.

She laughs. 'Everyone knows her. That's TJ.'

'Does she bring her bike here?'

'Doesn't have to. She can fix it herself. It's an old Triumph Trophy.' Dot's looking at me, and I'm looking away. 'Why do you want to know?'

'No reason.'

'I thought you weren't interested in … you know.'

'I'm not.' Now I'm blushing. *Damn it.*

'Not just a woman, but a foreigner. What would your mum say?'

I don't want to think about that. 'Oh, Dot, shut up.'

'She's way too old for you, too. Must be late twenties.'

'It's not like that. I just wondered. What does TJ stand for?'

'*Trouble,*' she says.

'And the J?'

'*Just beware.*'

'Very funny.'

'I'm dead serious. Look out.'

'I don't know what you mean.'

A silver Triumph Trophy is parked on the footpath outside Pellegrini's. I leave the Vespa a few yards up the street and give her a pat so she doesn't feel neglected. Smooth down my hair. Take a breath.

The window is steamed up. The door half-open. Inside, the café is packed, as always. A Frank Sinatra record plays. Everyone's shouting over the sound. Beatniks in berets. Rockers in jeans. Shop girls on a night out on the town, eating strudel and watching the boys. A poet puffing on his pipe and reading a small leather-bound book. Dot's in the far corner, talking with her mouth full. She waves to me, flicking spaghetti everywhere.

I call out across the bar to Signor Pellegrini.

'Could I have a cappuccino, please?'

He nods and turns away. The Gaggia gurgles.

Someone swings around on the bar stool right in front of me.

It's you.

TJ.

Trouble.

'He doesn't approve of people who have so much milk in their coffee,' you say. 'Let alone chocolate on top.'

You don't look at all like Annette Funicello up close. Or James Dean. I think I'm staring. I try not to, try to breathe and talk and maybe even smile, but your eyes are the most ridiculous green.

'I know it's not how they do it in Italy,' I manage to say at last. 'But I like it.'

'Don't worry,' you say. 'He doesn't like me much, either.'

I glance down. You're cradling a tiny espresso cup in one hand. The other hand rests on your thigh. I try not to look at you, at too much of you — look away — and there you are in the mirror, looking at me.

'But you …'

You smile. 'Oh, I drink coffee the way it's meant to be drunk. That's not why the *signore* disapproves of me.'

'Once he growled at me,' I say. 'He actually growled.'

'He doesn't like to see ladies wearing trousers.'

'My mum's the same. I had to sneak out of the house before she saw me.'

You shout something at him in Italian and he shouts back and, when you laugh, it echoes off the tiles. Everyone looks. At you. At us.

'Sit down,' you say.

'I'm meeting friends.'

'Go on,' you say. 'Or I'll growl at you myself.'

Your voice is like Sophia Loren in *Boy on a Dolphin*, like sparkling water and red wine and summer.

I sit down.

'You're the girl on the scooter,' you say.

'Yes, Audrey.'

Laughter bursts from you like fireworks. 'Truly?'

'Not me,' I say. 'I'm Nancy. My scooter is Audrey.'

'Naturally.'

A coffee slides across the laminex towards me. I hand over a shilling and Signor Pellegrini scatters the change on the bar.

I throw him a smile. 'Thank you.'

He's already back behind the Gaggia, polishing the chrome.

'He loves that damn machine,' you say. 'Like other people love their motorcycles.'

'No wonder he's proud of it.' I glance around the room. 'A café with a real espresso machine? Everyone in Melbourne wants to try it.'

You smile and tip your empty cup in my direction. 'Salute.'

'Audrey is a GS 150,' I say.

'I know,' you say.

'Can you tell that just by looking?' I ask.

'Don't be silly. I don't know a thing about Vespas. I asked Dot.'

'About Audrey?'

'About you.'

I stand there like a fool — you as smooth as a love song, and me not knowing what happens next or what to do or how to breathe.

'Drink your coffee,' you say. 'Let's go for a ride.'

Don't panic. 'I'm meeting friends, remember.'

'Who?'

I look around. 'Dot. And other people.'

'They're boring,' you say. You lean a little closer. 'But I am fascinating.'

I splutter into my coffee.

'Also, you have milk froth on your nose.'

The night is still warm. Breathless. You slide onto your motorbike as if you're made for each other.

I tie a scarf over my hair. 'Shall I follow you?'

'You won't be able to keep up.'

'Says who?'

'Leave Audrey here,' you say. 'Jump on the back.'

'Of yours?' It comes out as a squeak.

'I won't let you fall off.'

'It's not that,' I say.

'What then?'

'It's just …'

'What are you afraid of?' you say, so softly I only just catch it.

'Nothing.'

And everything.

'Don't be.'

And suddenly I'm not. I slip onto the saddle behind you.

The engine rumbles.

'Hold on to me,' you say, and I do.

You kick the stand away and wheel around to face down the Bourke Street hill.

'Let's go look at the stars.'

I just nod. I can't speak. You straighten up, throttle the Triumph into a roar, and we're off.

My arms are tight around your waist. We lean together into the corners, and forward against the wind — through the dark city, flying past the Tivoli and Myer's and all the way to Spencer Street, bumping across tram lines and bluestones, over the river, and passing my house where Mum and Dad sit in the kitchen watching *Pick A Box* and shouting at the television. Somewhere between the city and the beach, the scarf flies off my head and is lost in the night, my hair streaming behind me.

I can always smell the sea before I get to it — a memory of picnics and Calamine lotion and seagulls and laughter. You slow for a moment, then take off along the waterfront. I don't know what speed we're going and I don't want to know. Audrey never moves this fast. I never move this fast.

We don't try to talk. There's no point.

My body's so close to yours I can feel your ribs, your breath. Your heartbeat. Your thighs.

You slow to a crawl along St Kilda Beach, circle around past Luna Park and the St Moritz ice-skating rink, then pull up near the sea baths. There's nobody much about — a few couples huddled in the sand, their legs tangled together, and a man walking his dog along the pier.

'I love it here,' you say. 'Let's walk a little.'

My legs feel a bit wobbly after the ride. At least, I think that's why.

'Are you all right?' you ask.

'Of course.' Bright smile.

You put one hand in the small of my back and guide me towards the pier. The man with the dog is at the far end, near the kiosk.

'I wish it was open,' I say. 'I'd love an ice cream.'

'One day,' you say, 'I will bring you back here in the sunshine.'

I wonder if there will be another day. But for now, in the dark, we walk.

'How old are you?' you ask.

'Nineteen. You?'

'Older than that,' you say. 'Tell me, how can a young woman like you afford your own wheels?'

'I pay off a little bit every week.'

'Where do you get the money?'

'I work. Don't you?'

'Sure. You work in a bank?'

'Me? Goodness, no. Do I look like it?'

'Maybe. You dress so fancy. Capri pants. That cardigan.'

'All on lay-by from Myer's.'

'In an office, then?'

'No, I work on the trams. I'm training to be a conductress. My dad does, too. But he's a driver.'

'I wish I could drive a tram,' you say.

'Ladies aren't allowed to be drivers. But maybe Dad could take you for a ride in the cabin one day. I'll ask him.' As soon as the words come out, I know it's no use. Dad will take one look at you and decide you're a bad influence. Or a tomboy. Or worse.

'Where do you work?' I ask.

'In a factory, making uncomfortable shoes for rich ladies. My father works there, too. You see? We are the same, you and me.'

'Except your motorcycle goes a lot faster than mine.'

You laugh. 'That was slow. When I'm out on the open road — Ah! Then I go, fast as … as … I can't describe it.'

'Lightning?'

'Yes! That's it. But the bike is old now. I am saving all my money for a new one. A Harley Davidson.'

'Like Marlon Brando in *The Wild One*?'

'But prettier.' You chuckle and lean on the railing, peering into the water.

'I'm saving up to travel the world,' I say.

You look up. 'Why?'

'To have an adventure, before I get married,' I say. 'I want to go absolutely everywhere.'

You shake your head. 'Here is better.'

'It's all right for you. You grew up somewhere exciting.'

'Who says?'

'You're Italian.'

'But I have lived here for many years.'

'Since the war?'

You gaze out to sea.

'I suppose you've seen the wonders of Rome?' I say. 'The Forum, the Colosseum?'

'You have watched too many movies, I think.'

'I've read too many books. That's what Mum reckons. But you — you've really been there.'

'Not Rome,' you say. 'I'm from the north. Near Lucca. But we left when I was young. It was not exciting. It was not a good place. Not in the war. Not afterwards.'

'It's strange to think we would have been enemies in the war — your father might have fought against my father.'

'My father didn't fight against anyone. He was a farmer.'

'Mine drove trucks.'

'Was he in a battle?'

'A little bit. But not against Italians.' I don't actually know if that's true. He's never told us anything about it. And anyway, it has nothing to do with me, with you.

You offer me your arm. I slip one hand into the crook of your elbow. We walk on, our footsteps sounding hollow on the timber. We nod to the man with the dog.

'Lovely night,' he says. 'Don't get into any mischief, ladies.'

'We won't,' you say.

'Pity,' he says. 'I have wine at home. You're welcome to come share it with me.'

'No, thank you,' you say. You lead me away. He keeps

talking to our shadows.

'There's always one,' you say. 'Why is that?'

'He must be lonely.'

'Everyone's lonely,' you say. 'You don't hear us talking to strange girls in the middle of St Kilda Pier.'

'But that's exactly what we are doing.'

You stop, swing around to look at me. Even in the starlight, your eyes glitter green. 'We are not strangers. Not anymore.'

'I suppose not.'

We walk a little farther. 'His dog,' I say, 'looks just like that little Russian dog they sent into space. Just think. The poor wee thing is in orbit, all by itself, this very moment.'

'But imagine the view from up there.' You point at the moon, thin and pale as a fingernail. 'When are you getting married?' you ask.

'Me?'

'You said …'

'I just meant, generally.'

'But you will?'

'Doesn't everyone?' I say.

'I suppose so. Do you have a boyfriend?'

'No. Nothing like that.'

'Sweet sixteen and never been kissed?'

'I have so!'

'Really? By who?'

'Gregory Wallace.'

'Lucky boy.'

'In the back row of the Eclipse Theatre. If I remember rightly, it was a matinee of *Gentlemen Prefer Blondes*.'

You grin. You're staring at me. Too close. I bend down, pick up a broken mussel shell, and flick it into the water.

'Why are you asking all this?'

'Just curious,' you say. 'And that is it? Just the fortunate Gregory?'

'Do you think I just go around kissing people?'

'I don't know.'

We reach the end of the pier. It's a long way back to the shore. Below us, the high tide swirls around the pylons.

'If it was a bit warmer, we could go swimming,' I say. Bare legs in the dark water. Our bodies floating.

'Next time,' you say. 'Swimming and ice cream. I promise.'

'What about you?' I say. I try not to look at your throat, at your mouth. 'Have you kissed anybody?'

You throw your head back and laugh like a wharfie. 'Plenty of people. But that's not the question.'

'What is, then?'

You take one step closer. 'Who will I kiss next?'

I shuffle backwards. 'How can anyone ever know the answer to that?'

'I think I do.'

I turn away. There's a ship steaming out of the bay, horn blaring, lit up like Christmas — sailing to Perth, maybe, or London. 'Well, I suppose married people know.'

'Not always.'

I swing back around. 'What? Are you married, TJ?'

You take off your jacket and spread it on the pier. 'Come,' you say. 'Sit with me.'

'I should be getting back.'

'Yes, I am married,' you say.

'Who to?' I feel a bit sick inside at the thought of it.

'A mechanic. His name is Pietro. Peter.'

'Why aren't you at home, then?'

'Can't married people go out?'

'I suppose so. But it isn't—'

'Normal?'

'Yes. No.'

'I am not very good at being normal,' you say.

'I noticed.'

'You did?'

'There aren't many women who dress like you. Or ride motorcycles.'

'Please,' you say. 'Come sit.'

I lower myself onto the jacket, my feet folded under me. The night is colder now, darker somehow, and windy. We sit for a few moments, not looking at each other, just at the bay and the sky, the dark shapes of palm trees and yacht masts, and the city lights in the distance. Somewhere a dog yaps.

'I was married at sixteen,' you say, drawing the words out like a song. 'I was pretty then, with long hair like yours. I had a job in a shirt factory and Pietro worked in a garage around the corner. Every day when I walked to the tram stop, he whistled at me. He tried to talk to me, but I ignored him. Then he found out where I lived. He visited every Saturday and eventually everyone got used to him. He asked Papa for my hand, and Papa said yes. Nobody asked me.'

I want to say, *That's terrible*. I want to stroke your hair, your hand. I don't. I just sit there.

'He's a good man,' you say. 'Strong. Hard-working. But we make each other unhappy.'

'What's he doing tonight?'

'I don't know. He's in Bundaberg for the cane harvest. He lives there now, with a woman.'

'How awful!'

'Much better this way, believe me.'

'You don't mind?' I want to ask so many questions. But you're staring down at your hands, turning the Triumph key over and over in your fingers. No wedding ring.

'Nancy,' you say, and my name thrums like a song on your tongue. You look up at me and smile. 'Did you ever kiss a girl?'

'Of course not.'

You aren't smiling now.

'Dot has though,' I confess. 'She tried to kiss me once.'

'But you didn't let her?'

'No.' I'm blushing now in the dark. 'She's kissed lots of other girls, though. She told me.'

'And you are still her friend?'

'I've known her a long time. Since grade two. But one night she got a bit tipsy, and, well, she'd never told anyone else. She has other friends now — people like her. Don't tell her I said anything. It's supposed to be a secret.'

'It is safe with me.'

'I know.'

Silence. I can hear my own breath, ragged in the wind.

'Have you?' I whisper. 'Have you kissed a girl?'

'Yes.'

'Oh gosh — have you kissed Dot?'

You let out a laugh. 'Don't worry. She's not my type. And I'm not hers.'

'How do you know?'

A lopsided grin, just like Jimmy Dean. 'I feel it in my bones.'

'I don't have a type,' I say. 'Although I do quite like Elvis Presley.'

'Thought you might.' You flick your hair back off your forehead, Elvis-style.

'Love me tender,' you croon, sweet and soft. 'Love me true.'

It's my turn to laugh. 'I knew you'd be a singer.'

Now we're smiling, silly grins as wide as the moon, two girls drunk on nothing — on everything.

'Hello again, ladies.' It's the man with the dog. He's about as old as Dad. Hair slicked in grey strings over a bald patch. 'What are you doing out all alone in the dark?'

'But we aren't alone,' you say.

He doesn't take any notice. 'Mind if I join you?'

You scramble to your feet. 'Yes, actually, we do mind.'

'Don't be like that,' he says. 'I brought a bottle with me.'

You reach out your hand to me. 'We're just leaving.' You pull me up, grab your jacket and slip it on.

'Have a pleasant evening,' you say.

We try to walk away but he grabs my arm.

'Come on, love.'

'Let go of her.' You shove him away but his fingers dig deeper.

'You're hurting me.'

'Give us a kiss.'

You start yelling. 'Get your filthy hands off her.'

'Listen to me, darl,' he hisses the stink of cigarettes and stale beer into my face. 'You're too pretty to hang around with that *freak*.'

You stomp hard on his toes with your boot, and he yelps. The dog races in circles, yapping.

'Run!'

I fling him off me, and we race back to the road. His curses follow us. You leap onto the Triumph, cool as Jimmy Dean, and I wrap my arms around you. Then we're gone, free, roaring through the darkness, and we don't look back.

We never look back.

JORDI KERR

Jordi Kerr is an emerging writer who identifies as queer
and non-binary, and who lives with chronic illness — an
autoimmune disease affecting their muscles that requires
regular hospitalisation for treatment. Although they grew up
in a small country town where no-one was openly queer, they
now work in regional Victoria supporting LGBTIQA+ young
people. This story is a work of fiction, informed by Jordi's
own experiences. Jordi writes, 'There are many myths, and
misunderstandings (and tropes) about experiences of being part
of the LGBTIQA+ community. I wanted to touch on complex
aspects like hiding your difference, and inherited trauma.

I also really wanted to write about bodies. I've always had a
complicated relationship with my own body — firstly as a fat
person, then as a queer person, and then as a person with a
chronic physical illness. But I think feeling disconnected from
your body in some way, or feeling like you have no control over
it, is an almost universal experience. There's a lot in dominant
culture that says we should hate or be ashamed of our bodies,
but our bodies are our homes. I advocate for bodies as sites of
pride, kindness and love.'

Sheer Fortune

Everything is weightless. I float, I fall, I fly. It is quiet here —
no sound except the soft pulse of my own flesh, the gentle but
urgent thrum of my heartbeats.

I missed the ocean badly. Missed swimming in water that
wasn't brown and cloudy, where I could open my eyes
underwater without them stinging with grit.

Mum moved us here after what happened to my
Aunt Haven. She was in the news for weeks. Utterly
unrecognisable, of course. No-one except Mum and me had
any idea that the pieces of body they paraded in front of the
cameras belonged to Haven Krooksen. Not the fishermen
who found her, the police or the scientists. Definitely not
the media or rubberneckers, who I reckoned must have
descended from blowflies.

Mum decided that the ocean wasn't safe. She was all
up-anchors and set-sail for any town that had absolutely no
anchors, no sails, and definitely no water that connected to

the sea. So now me, Mum, and our collective grief are all in country hell. Also known as Warragowra.

I missed Aunt Haven too. A world without her seemed as impossible as a life without the ocean, and I don't actually know where the ache of one loss ends and the other begins. I do know that what happened to her wasn't the fault of the ocean. Not that I can even begin to have that argument with Mum. How d'you ask someone to look at both sides, when hers is weighted down with the body of her sister?

I stretch out … the edges of the dam are beyond my reach but they still feel too close. The sensation pulls at my nerves and the water shifts from being my support to being a weight, pressing against me from all sides. Tight, claustrophobic. I try to slow my movements, try to propel myself gently away from the panic.

Something wet flicked onto the back of my neck and giggles ebbed around the back of the room. I refused to turn around. Mr Stevens faltered a little in his explanation of *Moby Dick*, aware something was amiss, but unable to pinpoint exactly what. If I turned around, it would have cemented his suspicions and he would have pulled the class to a halt. Which would have given me an automatic downgrade from *stoic* to *snitch*.

'Brenna,' Mr Stevens said, calling on me.

Oh no.

'What ...'

Don't ask what's going on.

'... is ...'

Crap.

'... the importance of relationships within *Moby Dick*?'

Oh.

'Uh ... well, the dominant relationship in the text is unrequited.'

There was a whisper, 'She'd know a lot about that.'

'Go on,' Mr Stevens continued, flicking his hands to indicate he required a response longer than one sentence.

'Well, the book is all about Ahab and the whale, and the whale gets no say in any of this. The whole narrative is driven by Ahab's desires which're represented with some pretty damn phallic imagery. Really, the story can be read as symbolic of our patriarchal society — a white dude perpetuates a bloody dick-slinging match—'

'Language, Brenna.'

'Sorry, harpoon-slinging match, because he got told *no*.'

'That's not—' Mr Stevens began.

'She's right, Mr Stevens.'

I looked around. Marama had her hand raised and spoke with certainty, even though Mr Stevens hadn't called on her.

'The thrust of the novel is a cishet, white male's determination to literally plant his harpoon in a violent and retributive manner in a creature that he labels as wild and dangerous, simply because it didn't acquiesce to his whims. It holds a mirror up to a culture that values the desire of one person with privilege over the wellbeing of all others. It's colonial narrative meets revenge porn.'

More snickers from the heathens at the back of the room. Trent tried to start a slow clap. Mr Stevens silenced him.

'Cishet? What's that?' Billy asked.

'Ah. Yes. Marama, would you like to explain it to the class?' Mr Stevens dodged the question.

Marama turned in her chair to face Billy. 'Someone who is both cisgender and heterosexual. And if you don't know what those mean, I suggest you google them. It could be a highly educational experience for you.'

Marama made eye contact with me and grinned. It was the first time anyone here had done anything other than sling barbs at me.

'Thank you,' I mouthed silently.

'Welcome,' she mouthed back.

I sweep across the bottom of the dam, stirring up mud. It gives the water a burnt taste and there's a susurration from the disturbed yabbies. Everything about me is yellow brown grey and I don't know when this started or when it will end. Time is an eternity, a second. I keen for the pulse of waves and the endless blue and the chatter, chatter, chatter of other creatures.

Here there is no moment of seeing and being seen. No joyous intertwining with family. I am alone.

When I was twelve, my mum and Aunt Haven took me to the beach and gave me *The Talk*. I'm pretty sure it was a different version to what everyone else my age heard about changing bodies. In Health class at school, it was all about hair and involuntary secretions of blood and semen. My body, Mum warned, was going to start growing scales.

'I'm afraid you're a were-kraken,' she said.

It sounded so absurd I figured Mum was attempting her first ever practical joke and, predictably, failing hard. She was in full therapist mode, though — open body language, steady eye contact, kind tone, and a slight tilt to her head.

It didn't add up.

I looked at my aunt, who was nodding conciliatorily.

'I am too,' she said. 'And so was your grandmother. And her mother before her ...'

'It affects all those born female in our family,' Mum added quietly.

Haven wrapped an arm around Mum's shoulders and stroked her back as she continued. 'Mum — your grandmother, I mean, called it the family curse. The way she told it, Andreas, a fisherman ancestor of ours, killed a kraken because it was stealing his fish, and fed his family with it. They all died instantly — poisoned — except for his daughter, who'd refused to eat it. But the kraken got its vengeance on the whole family anyway because Erica, the daughter who didn't partake, was instead cursed to turn into a kraken during every full moon.'

'Which is all bullshit,' Mum said. 'But it was what our mum had been told, and it was how she reconciled the apparent impossibility of her own reality.'

'She also told the story much better than me. That was the CliffsNotes version. Your grandmother really got into it.'

'She was quite the storyteller,' Mum agreed. 'However flawed the story. How on earth did a fisherman manage to kill a kraken with just a spear?'

'Because he threw it with all of his anger!' Haven imitated my grandmother's voice.

'Oh, of course. *All of his anger!*'

'And by fortune—'

'*Sheer fortune.*'

'—pierced its brain.'

'May we never forget the mighty strength and sheer bad luck of poor fisherman Andreas,' Mum said soberly.

She offered me her hand, and I took it. I felt like I'd just lost something, but I had no idea what. I was still me. I was still right here, with Mum and Haven. Dune beneath us, waves in front.

So why was I crying?

'Mum?' My voice cracked and she wrapped me in a hug.

'It's okay. It's okay,' she repeated. 'We're here for you. We'll always love you.'

'I don't understand …' I sniffled. But even as I said it I knew that wasn't quite true. At the core of me, a song was stirring. Everything Haven and my mum had said sounded familiar, albeit in a distant way, like when my guitar aligns with my tuner. I felt the truth, and it was terrifying.

'What's gunna happen?' I asked instead.

Mum kissed me on the forehead. Cupped my face in her hands and looked me in the eye as she spoke. 'Haven will be with you every step of the way, okay?'

I looked at Haven, who nodded and smiled. 'It's hard,' she said, taking my other hand, 'Which sucks. But it's also beautiful.'

I propel forward, restless, hunting. There is nothing and no-one. I reach the dam wall. Flick back. The other end. Everywhere I turn wall, wall, wall. I thrash my tentacles. The surface of the water waves and froths, but they touch nothing familiar. There is no steadying curl from my kin.

Marama's head appeared as I was gathering up my headphones and sandwich. She rested her chin on my locker door.

'If you're going to be looking at gender in *Moby Dick* for your final essay we should work together.'

139

I stared. A group of younger boys barrelled past yelling about dibs on something.

'Sorry?'

'English? Taking down the patriarchy one essay at a time? You, me, together? The people united will never be defeated?'

'I'm not sure two students really count as a union.'

'All greatness has to start somewhere. What's that thing people say? If I throw rocks at people it'll make ripples?'

'Yeah, in that saying the rocks are kinda gently plopped into a pond as a symbol for one person creating change. It definitely isn't about throwing rocks *at* people.'

'Oh. That's a shame. People are so selfish and rude.' She chewed a fingernail absent-mindedly before adding. 'And *boring.*'

'I think squid are much nicer than people,' I blurted out. *Really, Brenna? That'll be another ten points in the weirdo column.*

'Yeah, they're pretty cool aren't they?' Marama said, apparently unfazed. 'I've seen the colossal squid in the museum in Wellington. It reminded me of the Taniwha. It's so beautiful, but seeing it like that … hunted and preserved and colourless. It made me incredibly sad.'

With a gut-stab, I wondered if pieces of Aunt Haven would be put on display in a museum. *Sea monster exhibit — grand opening!*

'You're from New Zealand aren't you?' I asked, instead.

'Yeah. So don't worry — I know what it's like to be the New Kid.' She winked at me, and added, 'Fish and chips. Piss off, ghost. Six, six, six.'

'Uhhh … what?'

'Accent requests. Figured I'd get it out of the way.'

'Oh. Yeah … What was that last one again?'

She saw my eyes flashing, laughed and jostled my shoulder. 'You're a cheeky one, aren't you?'

I still carry the echoes of that laughter in my heart.

I thrash again and again, the water churning, growing muddier, darker. Debris — leaf litter, bark — swirls and stretches for the edge of the water, just as desperate to escape me.

Two days later, I tried to contain my nerves while Marama poked around my bedroom.

'Cool gat,' she said, picking up my guitar.

'You know how to play?' She wasn't in the music class.

She sat on my bed, placed the guitar on her knee and proceeded to strum badly on the neck with one hand.

'Not. At. All. But how do I look?' She tossed her hair back and struck a pose.

She looked so sexy that my stomach flipped.

'Well,' I stalled. 'You look like you don't know how to hold a guitar properly …'

'Teach me!' She grinned and wriggled her shoulders in excitement. 'Please!'

Her joy was infectious. I smiled back.

She patted the bed next to her. 'I solemnly swear to be a diligent student.'

I ended up spending nearly an hour showing her how to hold the guitar and play different chords, all while trying to make as little physical contact as possible, which wasn't easy. When we finally moved onto English she had returned the guitar gently to its stand.

'Thank you,' she said, and placed her hand on my arm. Goosebumps rippled across my skin.

I float, motionless. There is no undulation to the water and little particles float in the moonlight. I taste some experimentally. It is not food. I think I am troubled by this, but I'm no longer sure.

Marama kept coming back. I couldn't find it in myself to tell her she shouldn't. To tell her to stay away.

She also insisted my place was a much better study environment. And after visiting her place, I had to admit she was right. Her family all had the same easy smile, and a warmth about them that made me want to sign up to be adopted by them. No offence intended to my Mum — I just figured we could *both* move in. I was pretty sure the Paratas would've been on board, too, but Marama already shared a room with her older sister, Meri, and her two younger brothers were frequent visitors. I thought all their questions were pretty sweet, but Meri kept screaming 'Pokokohua!' which Marama said was a threat to boil their heads, and chasing them out.

So we worked at my place.

'If you could be any character aboard the *Pequod*, who would you be and why?' Marama lay draped across my bed and sucked on a pineapple lollipop between philosophising on *Moby Dick*. I sat on the floor with my laptop.

'Pip,' I replied instantly.

'And why.'

'Cos given half the chance I'd jump into the ocean too.'

'Brenna?'

'Yup?' I responded, still typing.

'You're ridiculous.'

I looked up to fire back a retort. She was grinning at me. 'It's adorable,' she added. She slid onto the floor next to me. I could smell the sugar on her breath. The air felt thick yet fragile. My heart thrummed as we sat there, breathing together.

'Is it okay if I kiss you?' she asked softly.

I nodded, not daring to voice just how okay it would be. How I'd been falling asleep to the dream of what that might be like. And then her hand was on my neck, fingers curling into my hair. Her lips were on mine and it wasn't a dream — it was wet and real and more tender than I had imagined. I closed my eyes and fell gladly into this new world of ours. I let my hands slide around her, pulling her closer. She emitted a small moan of pleasure and the sound made my whole body ache in a way that I never thought would be possible with another person.

Listen. (Silence.) Move. (Wall.) Hunt. (Nothing.) Listen. (Silence.) Move. (Wall.) Hunt. (Nothing.) Listen. (Silence.) Move. (Wall.) Hunt. (Nothing.)

'We need to talk.' She pulled me aside in the school corridor and she wasn't smiling. My body had flushed cold and a wave of nausea gripped my stomach.

'Sure, what's up?'

'Where were you last night?'

My stomach cramped again.

'Whaddaya mean?'

'Don't you dare pull that shit,' she snapped. 'I came around to yours and *you weren't there.*'

'Marama, I told you I couldn't see you last night.'

'And I want to know what the hell you were doing last night. Because most people are at home at ten pm on a school night. Your mum certainly was! And she had no idea where you were. So how about you tell me?'

'I was—' I swallowed. 'I was—'

'Oh just spit it out. If you're interested in someone else just have the decency to tell me. I'm not a child — I need you to be honest with me.'

What could I have possibly told her?

I told her the truth. She refused to speak to me after that.

Nothing nothing nothing

I was lying on my bed listening to Tash Sultana sing my hurt when my door was flung open so hard it ricocheted.

'Brenna, what are you still doing here? Get to the dam *now*.' Mum's words were stern and her eyes were panicked.

I looked at the time ... I should have been waiting by the dam half an hour ago. *Oh no.*

I started to strip off some of my layers of clothing but Mum pushed me out of the room.

'There's no time. *Go*.'

She was right. The first convulsion hit and knocked me to my knees. Mum swore and helped me up, pushing, pushing.

'Quick! Run!'

I ran for my life, my mother behind me every step to the water's edge.

Something plunks into the water and falls away. A moment later, something does so again. A third plunk falls near me. I reach out a tentacle and grasp it.

It's a rock.

A shiver runs along my tentacles. A memory stirs within. I see a flash. A yellow lollipop. Black hair. I recoil, uncertain, afraid.

I'm torn into pieces, my body transforming back. The pain is, as always, unbearable. Every cell screams. Suckers become fingers. Limbs flap, flail, all my watery grace gone. Two hearts become two lungs and the pounding is no longer life but death, air desperate to break free. I purse my lips; try and capture it tight. My feet touch ground and I push against it as hard as I can. My head breaks the surface and I breathe like this is the life I want.

There are lights on in the house; the darkness of a person in front of them. The silhouette is too tall and angular to be my mum.

It's her.

My legs are shaking as I stumble out of the dam, and it's not just from unfamiliarity with this form. I have never been this scared before. My feet drag in the mud, the water drips off my naked body and I start to shiver so badly that I stumble and fall. I'm on my knees, staring at the shallows and not sure I can even lift my head to look again, when a blanket is draped over me.

Marama crouches down in front of me. Her dark eyes are steady and I ground myself in her gaze.

'Here,' she reaches out slowly, touching my arm, tracing around to my elbow. She guides me upwards, taking most of my weight.

She holds me, quiet, while my trembling subsides. When I'm able to stand stably, she looks at me and speaks.

'I'm really sorry, Brenna. I know that I hurt you, and I hope you can forgive me for being an egg.'

I take her hand, and entwine my fingers with hers.

'Absolutely,' I whisper, before I lean in and kiss her, our mouths merging like an ocean.

YVETTE WALKER

Yvette Walker is an award-winning novelist. She is a lesbian of Irish-Australian heritage. 'Telephone' is a fictional exploration of the difficulties she had as a teenager in coming to terms with her emerging queer sexuality. Yvette writes, 'The story is an imagined conversation between me and my younger self. I didn't want my story to be just focused on the difficulties of the coming out process. I think that's why it ended up being a conversation with the future; with a happier time and place. Without wanting to tell readers what to think, or how to read the story, for me, it's about courage. Looking back to my teenage self, I see someone who had a lot of courage; something I don't think I understood or recognised at the time. It's also about happiness. For centuries, gay, queer or lesbian life was written about as a life of unhappiness — I wanted the story to be about the everyday happiness of a lesbian woman.'

Telephone

The first call came at three-thirty in the afternoon.

Hello?

Hello, said a female voice, *can I speak to Kristin?*

There is no Kristin here, I said.

Oh, she was on last week — when is she coming back?

I'm sorry, there is no Kristin here.

Oh okay. Only, I called last week and Kristin told me to call back today. This is the gay and-lesbian-counselling-service? Only you didn't say. I checked the number … I checked the number five times before I called.

The voice was young, maybe sixteen, hesitant. I said to the girl, *No, this is not the Gay and Lesbian Counselling Service — but I am gay, actually, well, I prefer lesbian — would you like to talk to me? Would that help? My name is Yvette.*

Oh, said the girl, surprised. *That's my name too — Yvette. I'm Yvette too.*

And I knew the voice. And I knew the voice was me. I didn't know what to say.

151

Hello? said the girl, *are you there? Hello? My dad will be home soon. I'm using the phone in his bedroom and I have to be out of here in a few minutes.*

I sank slowly onto my bed. *Well, we should talk then*, I said to the girl, *for a few minutes, or however long you've got.*

I could hear the sound of the washing machine in my laundry, the sound of my wife mucking about with the washing, her whistling, the opening of the dryer door.

How are you? I said to the girl.

She found that funny. She laughed. I don't remember finding anything funny when I was her age — when I was her. I don't remember being able to laugh like that.

I relaxed a little. *Yes, sorry, you're calling a helpline, how good can you be? Let me try again. Tell me something about you, if you can. What's going on?*

There was a pause, as if the girl had left, and then, after a little while, she said, *I feel like I'm thirty-feet underground, in the dark. I can't talk to anyone. No one I know. Only Kristin, last week, and you now. You don't know me, so I can talk to you. Maybe you can help me. I don't know. But I can't stand it anymore. I can't breathe. I don't remember the last time I took a breath.*

That voice. The girl's voice. How did everyone not know this girl was in trouble? Were they imbeciles? Blind? The girl was radioactive with emotion. I nodded, then realised I needed to say something.

I said to the girl, *I understand, I do. I felt like that once. A long time ago. I know what you're saying.*

Then she said (to pivot away from the subject, that subject being herself) *What number is this?*

I didn't know what to tell her. Should I tell her that my telephone was the size of a cigarette packet, that my number began with 041 and was ten digits long?

Can I have your number? the girl said. *My Dad will be home soon and I have to, well, I have to make it look like I haven't been in here, that I haven't been using his telephone. I have to disappear. Can I have your number? I'd like to talk to you again, sometime, if that's okay.*

Yes, I said, not caring anymore that none of this was making sense. *It's a strange number,* I said, *but it will work. I don't know how you got through to me, but I'm glad you did.*

I gave her my number. She didn't question it. Then she thanked me, and she hung up. My wife came into our bedroom with a basket full of clean washing. She clocked the iPhone in my hand.

Anyone interesting? she asked me.

1987, I replied.

Yeah, right — good one Yvette, she said.

Our sixteen-year old selves were here first. Twenty, thirty years on, we still use the same heart that began with them. All of our doing in the world, all of our striving and working and building stems from that same heart, that unique heart that started beating so loud, we thought the whole world could hear it, too.

If it was a queer heart, if it was a loud, strong queer heart, then for some of us, for most of us, it felt, for a time, like hearing our own doom. On hearing that queer heart, on recognising it, we dreaded exposure, we wanted to be invisible. Yet the heart beat on anyway, without permission from us, without judgement. It was us, and we knew it without wanting to know it. In time, we would embrace this strange thing, this beautiful queer heart. We would. But we needed time, time to come to terms with that. But time, when you're sixteen, is so fast. We run, connections are made, broken, made again and we run, and everyone sees us, everyone knows everything, and we run, we watch others fall, we laugh at them, we mock them, and we run, packs merge and break apart, bones are broken, blood is spilt, friends are exiled and we run, we keep on running. Time, when you're sixteen, is so fast that bodies grow with it and through it, minds expand and hearts learn to beat loud, very loud; the world sings and we sing with it.

This is what it could be like, what it was like, sometimes, at sixteen, other times it was like being adrift in a small boat without a horizon in sight, not a clue how to proceed and everything was folly; meaningless and beautiful all at once, like the open sea.

The second call came about a fortnight later. I was building a fire in the wood burning stove. I'd split three barrow loads of cypress logs and I was sore from the effort. But the cypress smelt sweet and the bark smelt of earth and everything was good so I just got on with making the fire. Twisting the newspaper until it looked like ugly origami. Building a cage for the twisty paper, setting the big log on top of the criss-crossed kindling. Setting it all alight, letting it catch, closing the door but keeping the flue open. Then my phone rang.

Hello? I said. There was no caller ID. Nothing.

Hi, said Yvette. *It's me. Can you talk? I'd like to talk, if you can.*

This girl, this girl made my heart ache and I could barely breathe around it. *Sure*, I said. *Sure, we can talk.*

What are you doing? she asked me.

Building a fire. I've built a fire. It's cold here today.

The girl asked, *Where are you?* (Oh God, I thought, excellent question — I'm thousands of miles and thirty years away.)

New Zealand, I said to her. *I'm in New Zealand. And it's raining.*

Oh, the girl laughed.

That explains the strange number, the girl said.

Does it? I replied. *Good then. How are you?*

Ok, said the girl, when she plainly wasn't. Something had happened since we'd talked last. It could have been one of a dozen things, one of a dozen injuries.

Why can I talk to you? the girl asked me. *Why do I feel ok talking to you? Is it because we have the same name? And we sound alike. Have you noticed that? You have the same laugh as me.*

I said to the girl, *I know. I've noticed it as well. Tell me something. Tell me something about what is going on.*

The summer is going on, the girl said to me, *the summer won't end. I don't know what to do. I go to work, I buy records, I drive my car around, I go for a run. There are no more exams, I've passed them all. School is over. How can school be over? How can school end? My friends … Natalie has gone to Sydney with her family, and Shelley is still here but she's always busy, with what, I don't know. She's going to UWA next year, if she gets a place, science degree she says, even though she wants to make films. I'll get offered university places, my marks are good, but I don't know what to do. I don't know who to ask about it.*

No, I thought, you don't. No one is offering to talk to you. No one cares, but it will take you years to understand why. The girl lived like a ghost in her own house, almost invisible, always unseen. It was confusing. Bewildering. She couldn't think clearly.

And I'm on the other end of the line. Not being *her* anymore, and being an adult, I almost fall into the trap of

asking her *What do you want to do now you've left school?*
That ridiculous question that every generation asks its young
because they aren't honest enough to admit that no one has
a bloody clue, that few people understand what they want,
let alone how to get there, and we all settle, most of us, on
something less than our dreams.

And this girl is talking to me from before the internet,
before that gaudy narcotic display had become the source
of everything. All this Yvette has are pamphlets from the
school guidance counsellor (pie charts, flow charts, bullet
points) and some glossy University magazines, arriving in
the mail from various distant postcodes. I knew she was
interested in science, like her friend Shelley, that she actually
wanted to be an astronomer, that she could think of nothing
better than examining the Heavens, but she didn't have the
confidence to even try. Confidence had not been built into
her, no one had seen to that. She couldn't see that if she
tried, enrolled, that her physics and her mathematics would
be good enough, that her intelligence and work ethic would
see her through. It only occurred to her years later that it
would have only taken maybe ten per cent more effort from
her — then she could have got there. She was smart, she
knew that, a succession of teachers had told her so, but she
couldn't think. She didn't know how to make decisions about
her life — no one was steering her, guiding her.

I knew all of this. I knew only too well. How could I
change what had already happened? Did I want to? If I did,

what would happen to my present? To this life I had?

Doctor Who flashed through my mind. Where was the Doctor when I needed him? I guess this was too domestic for him, no Dalek invasion or creepy aliens eating up space and time like overgrown locusts. No world to save. Only my world. It was up to me. It had always been up to me.

Then the girl asked me, *Why are you lighting a fire in summer?*

I told her, *It gets cold here in the summer, it can rain all summer, you never know what's coming — a nice mild sunny day, or a miserable rain that makes your fish and chips soggy and your jandals wet.*

Jandals, what are jandals? the girl asked, laughing again.

Thongs, I said sheepishly. God, it was true, we Australians knew nothing about New Zealand.

Have you got a girlfriend? the girl asked me.

Yes, yes I have, I said. *Well, she is my wife actually. We're married.*

You can get married in New Zealand? the girl asked, not quite believing me.

Yes, yes you can, I said, without a word of a lie. I was thirty years away from her, and it was true. It was.

We've been married for eight years, together for thirteen years, I told the girl. I heard a sharp intake of breath. She must have thought I was from another planet.

I knew she hadn't met another gay girl yet, let alone kissed one (she would, in a year or so, kiss a girl, in her car, on a rainy night) and here I was, married.

What's it like, the girl asked me in a whisper, *what's it like to have a girlfriend?*

What a question. And I didn't want to lie and I didn't want to tell the truth either. I wanted to say that everything was marvellous and that we loved each other so much, that we never fought, that we never went to bed mad with one another and there were no problems, ever. I wanted my adult queer life to be perfect for her. I knew how romantic her outlook was, that was what comes with no one telling you anything or paying any attention to you, you have to fill in the gaps yourself, and she filled in the gaps with romantic notions of BBC actresses and swashbuckling sports stars who would fall in love with her at a glance. I knew these romantic notions would last far too long, into early adulthood, and she would get into trouble carrying around all that naivety.

How could I show her the kernel of marriage? Is that what she even wanted right now? Not everyone wanted marriage, needed marriage, queer or straight. I knew, right now, all she wanted was to hold hands with a girl, kiss her. She had no clue about sex with a woman because there was no information, sanctioned or otherwise she could access, and besides, she was too frightened to even think about sex too much. The feelings overwhelmed her. Better to daydream about meeting a rakish, charming woman in some English manor house, a no-nonsense, forthright woman who would take a liking to her. What could I tell her about the real world of queer love? That women could be cruel, duplicitous, manipulative? That sex and love rarely met? That dating was fun (yes), that sex was fun (yes) but love — love was complicated, beautiful, unique as a fingerprint, dangerous, difficult, a peculiar type of effort over days, years, and decades.

I was getting off track. The girl had asked me about having a girlfriend, not marriage, they were two very different things.

At first, I said to the girl, *it's enough to hang out with gay girls, it's enough to talk with them about who you like, who might like you, that's fun, that's the group you want now, right now, but you won't get them for a while yet, you've got to go out and find them — when you're ready, when you can. Then,* I said to the girl, *the next thing is to ask a girl out, or let her ask you out, it really doesn't matter, as long as it happens. And this is the first awkward stage, as sometimes the girl says no, and sometimes you say no (you can say no — you don't have to go out with a girl just because she has asked you), and you have to get used to being buffeted about a bit, between the longing and the wanting and the not quite getting. It's all fine, it's all normal, it's all part of it.*

So, the queer friends are more important, I said, *it's the queer friends that will get you through, those queer girls you love fiercely but you'd never go out with them (and when you try it's a disaster), that's who you'll remember with great fondness later on, they are who really matter in the end. And you know what's really nice*, I add, *what I really loved when I finally came out? I could go to a party, or a dance, or a nightclub and I could just look at girls. The freedom to look at girls, that was the most wonderful thing, the most liberating thing of all.*

Don't worry, I said to the girl finally, *you will have a girlfriend. A few, probably, that won't be so difficult, in the end. Don't worry.*

The girl didn't know what to say to all of that. She lived to worry. Her life was all about worry. Too much silence. Too much isolation. It made a person afraid, unable to move. After a time, she said, *Wow, that helps. Thank you.*

Thank you, I said.

She laughed. *For what?* she asked me.

For everything, I said. She'd saved me. She didn't know this. Without her, I wouldn't be kneeling by a wood burning stove in a farmhouse in New Zealand, feeding cypress into a fire. The girl was me, and I was the girl. Her sadness was mine, and my happiness was hers.

The girl asked if she could call again sometime.

Call again, Yvette, I said. *Call whenever you like. I'll be right here.*

The girl said she would. Then we said goodbye. My wife

was out in the garden. I could see her walking through the trees, the cat and the dog following. I would make her a cup of tea soon. We would chat about the day. The gratitude I felt for her love, expressed day after day in the simplest of moments, was without measure.

MELANIE RODRIGA

Melanie Rodriga, Antipodean film-maker and emerging author, was born in Kuala Lumpur, Malaysia and is of Eurasian (Malay-Chinese-Portugese) ancestry on her mother's side and British ancestry on her father's. She has lived in Malaysia, Australia, New Zealand and the United Kingdom. She describes her sexual orientation as fluid, and currently identifies as lesbian or queer. Her story relates to her extended family and its relationship to the broader questions of their heritage and is a contemporary take on her own experience of high school in Sydney, in the 1970s. Melanie writes, 'I wanted to challenge the assumption that sexuality is biologically or genetically driven. I believe that allowing young people the freedom to make up their own minds about their sexual preference(s) is the most important thing.'

DNA

Sunday. Lunch. Dad's place.

He's lived in this flat in Rose Bay since my mum divorced
him last year. It's small, but has a vintage-retro sort of vibe
plus it has a garden, which is good because there are a few of
us at these lunches. Dad's side, this is.

Mum's side (the Asian side) has lunch every other
Sunday. The two sides have never mixed all that much.
Maybe Boxing Day or something. It's always awkward.

So at Dad's, it's usually me (Michelle), my younger
brother Adrian and older sister Julie, Auntie Susie (Dad's
sister, also divorced), Uncle Neville (Dad's bro, also divorced
— I should just put 'a.d.' after all references to adult family
members on Dad's side) and whichever cousins turn up.
Blonde freckled ones who have usually come straight from
Bronte or Maroubra, or wherever the waves are.

Me and Adrian and Jules are not blonde and freckled and
we are not lovers of the beach, although Julie has been in the
swimming carnival maybe twice, and I will get sand in my

shoes if there is ice cream involved. Adrian is too young to know what he wants, except about getting his own way with everything. I see a great future ahead of him. Not so much me. I'm supposed to start uni next year and haven't even chosen a course. Something in science maybe. Dad says we can do anything, and be anything, but I'd like to see him try to navigate Sydney Uni's friggin' useless website.

Sunday. Lunch. Our place.

There are, like, way more people at this lunch because Mum's five sisters and their SUV-loads of kids *all, always* come unless there is an avian flu epidemic or a mob of them are in Singapore or KL or at the Buddhist temple in Wollongong. Our house — the house Dad doesn't live in anymore — is awesome. Dad inherited it from his parents. I never got to know my Anglo nana-pops, but their house is in the Eastern suburbs since it was a place where people with average money could live. From the deck, you can look at the Harbour for real, which is good, because phones are not allowed at lunch. So we look at the view (you get blasé after a while) and look at the food (never blasé about that) and look at each other and I have to say, we are a handsome bunch.

 If Dad's family are the blonde and sandy part of the Aussie gene pool, Mum's family range from half-brown types to jet black hair and pale skin. I'm an in-between one, a bit of everything. When Sunday lunch is at Mum's, she always puts oranges in front of the Kuan Yin statue in the hall and lights a joss stick to make her sisters think she's devout. Her Kuan Yin statue is really old. It belonged to Mum's grandmother, who brought it over from Penang where she said she found it in an antique shop (so it must be ancient) and my mum kind of looks after it for all the sisters.

There are extra flowers in front of Kuan Yin today as this lunch is for my Auntie Rose's fiftieth' and there are flowers on the table too. Rose is the least devout of the sisters, so there is a greater possibility of fun, and even outrage. Today she has brought a new boyfriend, Len, whom she found on some business trip in Thailand. Len is Vietnamese, but they talk Thai to each other, which is cool, if a little overwhelming. I have no Thai, no Mandarin, no Cantonese. Heck, I barely have English. Thank the Goddess of Mercy I have science.

Monday. Chemistry.

My teacher is Mr Yeo. ('Yo, Yeo'. 'Yo! Yo!').

I like his class (I like him), but then today he shattered my high expectations by bringing up Harry Potter. In chemistry. Why do teachers think that if they use a Harry

Potter example we'll understand stuff better? Mrs Delaskie did it in English, some 'Goddess Hermione' thing; but she had a point in that Hermione saved Harry and Ickle Ronnie *so* many times and yet Potter is the hero? Not Hermione?

Anyway, Mr Yeo used a muggle-wizard, full-blood-half-blood-mudblood reference in order to talk about genetics and DNA. Aka deoxyribonucleic acid, which not only makes up chromosomes but accounts for genetic characteristics in pretty much all, well *all*, life forms. It's a kind of spiral ladder of nucleotide strands with rungs of purine and pyrimidine, all carrying everything we have been and ever will become. 'DNA is what makes us who we are,' says Mr Yeo. Awesome, really.

It took great skill on Mr Yeo's part, I thought, to keep the discussion on-topic. Yet, in all his Harry Potter comparisons he never mentioned that Voldemort is actually a muddie. Like me.

Sunday. Lunch. Dad's place again.

The shit hit the fan, as Dad would say.

In fact, he did say it, right after freckled cousin Glen thought it would be funny to say 'Asians are so soy.' Anyway, Glen thought he was being super-ironic but he didn't know he'd just *truly* insulted me and ma sibs. And then all the freckled cousins joined in, 'Asians are soy, Asians are soy,' and we suddenly had a racial incident on a massive scale. People were leaping up out of their chairs.

'Dude, don't go there!' Adrian warned Glen, grabbing a bit of his shirt. So Glen and Adrian were about to take it outside when Dad started in on Uncle Neville for raising Glen *the wrong way* and then Mum arrived to pick us up, Mum had an extra go at Dad and then Mum, Adrian, Julie and me are sitting in the car fuming and Mum says, 'What's this *Asians are soy* business?' and Adrian says, 'It means *fucked*, Mum. Cousin Glen meant Asians are *fucked*.'

Sunday. Lunch. Auntie Grace and Uncle Stephen's place (and Stephanie and Michael and Wendy as they're home from, respectively, uni, uni, travelling the world).

Auntie Grace is the best cook of all the sisters. She even makes Uncle Stephen do his own barbecue duck as the great place in Chatswood is not up to her standards.

There was a bit of tutting about the racial incident at Dad's last week and then we moved on to the mediaeval topic of marriage equality. Auntie May burst in late at that point — she'd come straight from Temple — and was all fired up about marriage equality because she's always been against it.

Auntie Rose then accused Auntie May of being a

conservative mainlander so, Auntie May, spotting my new rainbow fringe, turned on me instead and hissed, 'Why don't you even have a boyfriend yet?' Everyone went quiet for a moment.

Then I shot back, 'Why identify as sexuality- or gender-anything when *nothing* is set in stone?'

It's the DNA image Mr Yeo showed us in class. It got me as fiery as Auntie May as I told her, 'I mean, look at the stuff DNA is made from, it has no beginning and no end. And if DNA is the basis for everything, then how can anything be for always?'

Adrian likes to challenge Auntie May as well, so he stuck up for me at that point and the shouting really began. I tried to shift Auntie May to the safer topic of the relationship between language, gender and sexuality. You can't separate them, incidentally — Google it and see — 'But can you always keep them together,' I said, 'and do we really have to?'

Auntie May wouldn't be distracted though, and went on and on about how *marriage should be natural* this, and *families should be natural* that, and I'd wanted to scream at her, '*I*'m natural! *I*'m as natural as you are!' But I didn't.

When I think about that twisty-turny DNA strand, I think of Voldemort again and how he disintegrates right at the end of *Deathly Hallows 2*. He turns into tiny particles that fall apart and just float away and it's kinda slow and beautiful and haunting (Bellatrix falls apart faster and sharper, more like glass) but it's also really, really, awful. *I'm* feeling it, and I realise I've been feeling like that for a while now, that I'm made up of tiny particles that are falling apart in a slow and mysterious fashion.

Wednesday. Chemistry.

Mr Yeo looked good today. Not as good as Mrs Yeo though. I was moping in the corridor after school and it turned out we were *both* waiting to see Mr Yeo. So me and Mrs Yeo had a chat. And she's looking at me with this look on her face and I just know, because I know that look, that she's asking herself, *Is Michelle* Asian? While I'm looking at Mrs Yeo and I'm thinking, *Am I* attracted *to her? Am I attracted to her* because *she's Asian and she reminds me of one of my aunties, and is that a bad/weird thing?*

Meanwhile she's saying to me, 'Mr Yeo says you're all studying DNA now,' and I am not really listening because I'm still staring at her but I say, 'Yeah — I mean yes. But he never actually said Voldemort is a mudblood … which is a gap in our learning I think …'

And I study the colour of her eyes. Blue. No one on Mum's side has blue eyes. This is quite disarming. 'Your blue eyes,' I say, 'did your ancestors live near the Black Sea eight thousand years ago?'

She laughs and says Mr Yeo should stop using the eight-thousand-year-old blue-eyed Black Sea Asians as a teaching example and we talk about our real ancestors for a bit — hers from Hong Kong, mine from Singapore and KL and Sydney.

Sunday.

Sunday lunch at Dad's does not happen this week. The Soy Wars are still raging. I have to feel for Dad. Although it was his brother and nephews who were out of order, Mum makes it all his fault, all the time. Listening to them shouting on the phone, it's like we are back in the break-up days, when they were falling apart and taking us with them. Little things became that much bigger than they should've because you couldn't think of anything else except the incomprehensible fact that your world was ending. It kind of layered over everything with an explosive effect — loud noises, angry colours, lots of missile-like debris that made your brain unable to function at anything beyond survival level.

Today their argument moves from their own shortcomings to how *fucked-up* their kids are. Never Julie, who is a jewel among girl-children; just me and Adrian, my smart and beautiful little-bro, who might be *queer*. And they talk about our flaws even though it was *their* DNA that produced us after all.

So, no Sunday lunch at Dad's. When he comes to collect us kids, he acts like the shouting match with Mum never happened and he takes us to a film in town and tells jokes and tries his best to makes us feel as normal as a broken family with one princess and two almost-certainly queer kids can be.

Monday. Chemistry.

So I ask Mr Yeo, straight up, 'Mr Yeo, you said that DNA makes us who we are? Then how does DNA cause people to be *not* heterosexual?'

I swear, all at once, everyone turns to look at me. It's scary, like some thirty-headed Nagini staring at me, just waiting for Voldemort to say 'Kill' the same way he'd say 'Walkies'.

Mr Yeo is confused, as if he just doesn't understand the question, so I ask it differently. 'Well, you know how some people use science to say that LGBTQI people are freaks of nature, well what is it about nature that makes non-LGBTQI people the way they are?' Then I get a bit fiery again and add, 'and if it is so natural to be hetero then why are there *a*-sexual people and why ...'

But before I can finish, Dion Kovanis says 'WTF is this LGBTXYZ shit anyway? Why not just say faggots and muff— ' and before *he* can finish Mr Yeo cuts him off by saying, 'That's enough Dion. Michelle has an interesting question, I think.' And Mr Yeo is tilting his head, looking at me and all the Naginis are still looking at me and why do I feel like I'm the only person in the room who's thought of this stuff? Then Mr. Yeo says quietly, 'Go on, Michelle.' So I take a breath and I do.

'DNA has no bias. It has no agenda. DNA doesn't tell us what to think. DNA doesn't control our behavior. It doesn't have to come out. Also, if we have cisgender like it's some birth-induced DNA thing, then why don't we have the term cissexual, which we don't?'

Some of the class have turned back, but most of them still stare like I'm raving and maybe I am, but I think about this stuff all the time because it's who I am. *It's who I am. Isn't it?*

Mr. Yeo nods, so I go on, even though I'm getting angry. 'If we have asexual why not just use the term 'sexual' instead of lesbian or trans or whatever? Gender is a sense; it's not science. Sexuality is behavior; it's not science.' And now it feels like my words are coming out all wrong and I can feel my face going a little red and my breathing is faster and my chest is tighter and my brain feels like its going to burst.

And I see Voldemort disintegrating into those countless fragments of his no-love skin and bone, bits of his sociopathic self shattering, dark, light, power-obsessed, that weird almost-nose, no-light eyes, no-hair, blood, half-blood kill all mudbloods, hating but snake-loving, each part reduced to dust until nothing, not even a

must-not-be-named atom remains. And I feel that I may
be falling apart too. Countless Michelle fragments of skin,
bone, whitish-brownish-yellowish, Asian, Australian, caring,
hurting, not-surfing, science-loving, whatever-sexual,
whatever-blood, it all starts to fracture and fly away because
I cannot hold it together anymore.

But it's kind of liberating. I imagine those little strands of
DNA, not flying away but bending and twisting and flexing.
All the little strands that make my hair brown and my eyes
hazel and my skin olive and my heart strong and my teeth
straight and I know that DNA does not make my choices
for me. I do that. I will tell me what kind of person I am and
what I think and how I live and who I marry or not marry,
who I love or do not love.

I am not falling apart. I am moving forward, always —
three minutes ago before I spoke in class, last Sunday when
I was under attack from Auntie May, the Sunday of the Soy
Wars, the week my parents divorced all the way back to
when I made my first best friend, whose name was Scott, by
the way, and he moved to Adelaide and we still send each
other birthday gifts.

And out of all that, something comes right to the front.
I remember saying to Auntie May, 'I mean, look at the stuff
DNA is made from, it has no beginning and no end. And if
DNA is the basis for everything, then how can anything be
for always?' and I realise that it can't and everything changes,
including me and everything in my world. And I know that

what matters is not what my DNA makes me, but what I make of it.

RAFEIF ISMAIL

Rafeif Ismail is a Perth-based, emerging Muslim writer who is a refugee from Sudan identifying as queer. While the story is fiction, parts of it were inspired by true events, personal experience and the desire to see more representation of queer, black Muslim women in fiction. Rafeif writes, 'I hope the story highlights that there is no single refugee story, queer story, migrant story, African story, Muslim story, etc. The danger of a single narrative is that it leaves individuals vulnerable to the dehumanisation that is at the core of all institutions of oppression.'

Almitra Amongst Ghosts

Houah Maktoub, your grandmother always used to say, *It is written.* She firmly believed that everything that will ever happen had already happened, that distance and time were no obstacle. You used to sit by her side, in the shade of a veranda overlooking a courtyard, in that house surrounded by tall walls painted white, with its metal gate that was green with age, always open. You listened, your fingers sliding across the imperceptible thorns of the okra you handed her, which she expertly cut for that night's dinner as she told stories she had grown up learning, in the village on the island between two Niles. Stories of family, friends and legends, she had weaved them together like a dark Sahrazad. It is where you first heard of Mohamad, the village boy who lived on the edge of the savanna, who cried, *Tiger! Tiger! Tiger in the grassland!* Until no one believed him, and his whole village was massacred as a result. Of Fatima, who sang so sweetly that a ghoul stopped the Nile for her, so that she may retrieve her lost gold. And of the spirits in the rivers, those on land and ancestors who whisper in dreams, reaching out from some other world with warning and advice. Years later, you will learn that quantum entanglement posits that two objects may exist in reference to each other regardless of space-time, and think on how much physics sounds like your grandmother's folklore and faith. At her side you learned of a world three parts unseen and believed in it. Now those days seem hazy and distant, and there is a space in you that twinges like phantom limb, as though you lost something you did not know you had, somewhere along the invisible borders between what you thought was home and here.

*

Your house is like every other, with three bedrooms, a kitchen and a living room, and your house is full of ghosts. You see them pass across your father's eyes as he stares at a wall, seeing a place that is not there anymore. They follow your mother into the sunlight as she gardens, they inform the heaviness of her step, the creaking of her bones. She is trying to grow chili, aloe vera, and a lemon tree — much smaller than the one that grew in your old home — that doesn't seem to want to flower. You see the ghosts on your way to the bus stop, where every day without fail, in the space of a single step, the street becomes dusty and you can smell sandalwood in the air. It is almost as though if you walk down that road, you will see your grandmother, sitting outside that green metal gate with a big wooden bowl at her feet, cutting okra. The ghosts thankfully don't follow close behind you at school, although they linger at the edges of the classroom, and in the shadows of the trees dotting your school oval. You get used to them over time, those flashes of scent, of memory, and you learn how not to react the same way you learn not to hide under your bed when you hear fireworks, or jump every time a car backfires. The dreams are more difficult to control but as the years pass you form an understanding between yourself and those haunting you.

*

It is 2016 and your newsfeed has been full of stories from the Orlando massacre, and suddenly the world is tilting much further along its axis, and gravity seems much stronger, every breath feels like a battle. You do not attend the vigil to commemorate the victims and survivors. You cannot bring yourself to leave your house. Adrift from your body, you feel trapped, unable to look away as the news shows people becoming hashtags, becoming tombstones. You finally understand why your mother cried that day two years ago, when you, eighteen and giddy to the point of intoxication, tried to find the words to explain something you did not have the language for, when you tried to tell her about Dunya.

'Everyone feels this way about their friends at some

point!' she had screamed, when you'd both lost your tempers — yours in frustration, hers in something closer to desperation. 'It does not mean you act on it.'

In your stunned silence you had offered no response.

'This will pass,' she had said, 'and we'll talk no more about it.' Ending the conversation. The distance between you grew, until now, where it feels like you are standing on opposite shores of the same river.

Now you see her words for the plea and prayer they were. There is so much that is unspoken in that ghost house of yours, the silence is often straining to burst as it rings on every wall. But, like bullets, words can ricochet and fragment, so you all keep your silences. You had called Dunya earlier that day, tired of navigating minefields in your living room. She had deactivated her social media accounts earlier that week, always much more practical when it came to dealing with grief, better at avoiding it, putting up walls and daring it to come closer. You, on the other hand, soak it up like injera does mullah, your comfort food, until it becomes all you can taste. Travelling to meet her is the first time you are out in the sun in days and everything is just a bit too bright, the bus crowded enough that you have to sit next to someone.

*

It is sometimes easy to fall into the dream of this country, to walk towards that mirage of blind equality and for a moment forget that your life has always been shaped by the actions of others, from centuries and continents ago to just now, as you step onto a bus and strangers with frightened eyes uncomfortably avert their gaze and shift as though shielding themselves, praying you don't come near them. As always, your embarrassment comes unbidden, rushing through you, prickling your skin like tiny okra thorns and your every movement automatically becomes an apology. You remember that so much of you is not your own. *Maktoub.* But not the way your grandmother believed. No, in this nation people assume they can write your story from beginning to end, and wait for you to fall into place on the stage that has been set. It is why every conversation scans like a hostage negotiation, with your humanity being the item that's up for deliberation.

Once, when you were fourteen and Dunya was still just one of the many girls you meet in passing twice a year during an Eid barbecue and your futures were not yet this possibility, there was a boy who walked home with you every day after school. You talked in a way that you never did on campus. Those conversations became the very best part of your day. He was different and made you laugh. He called you beautiful, for a black girl, and you kissed him. It would not be the last time someone would pay you a provisional compliment, nor the last time you accept it. Back then, you had not yet realised that those who viewed your beauty

conditionally, undoubtedly felt the same towards your
humanity.

  With Dunya, you found a love without stipulations and
it was at once both a revelation and revolution. She walks
proudly in the streets with her dark hair beneath brightly
coloured hijabs so obviously herself and it terrifies you
that she may not come back one day. As report after report
makes its way onto your newsfeed of attacks on women who
look like her — like you — you pray more fervently than you
have in years. Even if you're not sure who you are praying to.

It's one of those dime-a-dozen, cannon-fodder days that
roll on lazily through the summer, with a too hot sun
and clear skies, when you meet her, under a jacaranda
tree in some park you'd found when exploring the city
— its biggest attraction is that it's located several suburbs
away from where you both live. You have both learned to
compromise. You speak English with American accents
and Arabic with Australian ones. You hold hands but only
in places where you cannot be seen, because gossip spreads
faster than bushfires and neither of you would survive
the burn. Yet in those compromises of all that you are,
you still carve out spaces for yourselves. You sit for hours
under the shade of that tree, and remember stories from
an ocean ago, and Dunya reads out loud from her favourite
book. You listen to the cadence of her voice, as she recites
poetry the way she was taught to recite prayer. It is almost

undistinguishable from singing.

And there is a way to describe this moment, the shade, the tree, the breeze; this brief respite from the world — in the language you were both taught as children — *Al dul al wareef.* There is no comparable phrase in English. That is fine, there are no words for who you both are either in the language of your grandmother and your parents — the one you now speak with an accent. In that language love is described by forces of nature, monstrously destructive and divine, and in all of that is possibly an explanation as to why its words for breath and love are indistinguishable by sound. It is probably why songs only croon phrases like 'You are the Nile', 'She is like the Moon' and 'You are the *hawa* coursing through my veins'.

'So speak to us of love, said Almitra,' Dunya quotes in Arabic. Stories like yours don't have happy endings, not any you have seen. But you are not only beautiful in your tragedy. One day you will write this story, and speak of love; it might be read under a different sky, it might have a happy ending. *Just for now though*, you think, your eyes drifting shut, *I can keep living it.*

OMAR SAKR

Omar Sakr, Arab-Australian poet, editor and emerging author based in Western Sydney, is a half-Lebanese, half-Turkish, bisexual Muslim man, raised in a Lebanese family. This story is a work of memoir about kinship and the author meeting his Turkish half-brother for the first time. Omar writes, 'While I am attuned to the various nuances of being in specific spaces, politically I aim for solidarity across the spectrum of all the communities to whom I belong. I am disinclined to align with halves, and so seek the whole.'

The Other Son

I first met Attila in the Turkish funeral house where our father's body was being washed and prepared for its final bed. Chairs lined the walls of the large square waiting room, one filled by Babbanne, another by my aunt Yasmine, and three by my sisters Gulsah, Tugba, and Sumi. Several other miscellaneous older women drooped in their seats looking like sad bulldogs wrapped in blankets. The tacky red rug on the floor was an unnecessary reminder of blood in a place flooded with it. Attila stood in the empty space in the middle. He was unmistakeably a boy — slight, his hair thick and wavy, his body somehow casual. I was standing outside, looking in through the bell-shaped doorway, separated from him by two metres, a decade, and an affair.

A harried, bearded man poked his head out of the office opposite the waiting room, and reeled me in with his eyes. He said something in Turkish, the slurping sound of which I was at least familiar with, if not the meaning, and I stared at him.

'English, sorry,' I said.

He frowned. 'You knew the deceased?'

'I'm his son,' I said.

'Aha,' he said, picking up his pen. 'Was he married?'

'I don't know,' I said.

'How old was he?'

'I don't know,' I said.

He glared. 'You knew the deceased?'

'I … I'm his son.' I shrugged, helpless, and backed away from the door. The man came out babbling, but at the same moment my uncle Sedat stepped in from the cold where the men were gathered, letting me off the hook. Relieved, I rushed into the waiting room. I swooped onto Babbanne who was keening and rocking on the spot, interrupting her with my kisses, and then moved through the others one by one with a series of swift pecks on wet cheeks. My autopilot greetings stuttered into awkward silence around Attila, before finally I moved past him, and on to our sisters, who I at least knew. Gulsah, the eldest, held her newborn up like a shield to keep everyone at bay. Tugba came next and seemed more selfie than person, every hair immaculately arranged, a shining light brown crown. Sumi, the last of the girls, was younger than me and the donkey of the family, working twice as hard as everyone else. She was only twenty-five, but defeat had already stamped its fist on her round, kind face.

I sat next to her, and listened to them talk. Attila kept walking back and forth in front of us, constantly flipping his iPhone around in one hand, until I pointed at the chair next to me and said, 'Sit'. He flopped onto the seat without a word, like he'd only been waiting for a direction. He had faded light blue jeans on, and one of those stupid puffy jackets, khaki green. He leaned over in his seat, staring at the ground, the dark mirror of his phone highlighting his pale face, his sharp jawline. He was prettier than our sisters, even though his nose was as big as a baby's fist. It worked for him in a way that it didn't for the rest of us. It worked for him like it once worked for our dad.

Our knees were almost touching, but he might as well have been in another country. I wanted to stare at him forever, kept sneaking looks, kept opening and closing my mouth. How do you talk to a brother you've never known? Everything I could possibly say to him ran through my head and all of it was dumb. I told myself it wasn't my fault that a dead man's hand was covering my mouth. Attila's screen lit up with a notification. I seized on the light, taking the phone from him, dizzy with the force of sudden revelation.

'This is my number,' I said in an undertone, tapping it in. 'Call me whenever you want, okay?' He nodded slowly, then called my phone so that I had his number, too. I let out a long breath. Nothing separated us anymore.

I slept in Attila's bed that night.

When my sister Sumi suggested I stay with them I barely put up a fight. Truthfully, I was so hungry to know them, it scared me.

'What about your mum?' I asked. Her mum, like my own, had never been keen on us all mixing. 'What will you say?'

'I'll say: Omer's staying with us tonight. She won't care.' I love the way Turks say my name, a soft 'er' sound on the end making it a purr. Not like the Arab family I grew up with, who make it a hard 'ar'. Sumi was right about her mum not caring. Though she and I wouldn't speak for days yet, she didn't batt an eyelid at my staying with them. I guess after nearly thirty years I was an old sin, a scar past hurting. For her and for my mum, at least. Their place was a new duplex in Guildford, a shiny display house, and it was packed full of Turks. For the next six days, seemingly every relative or random person who had come into contact with my father, paraded through with their families to pay their respects. It was mayhem, with at least sixty kids at any given moment running around hounded by parents shouting their names, while separate clumps of men and women sat in the lounge ignoring each other. Like Arabs, whenever a Turkish family comes together, in grief or joy, it can only be described as a riot.

Attila spent most of his time with his cousin Orsun, another teen boy. From my seat at the men's table, I only caught glimpses of him flitting through the crowded house like a dream. After a while sitting amongst the older men, who wouldn't or couldn't talk to me except to say, 'Masha'Allah, you have his face, you are him exactly,'

I disentangled myself and went upstairs. It was dark out, dinner was done, it was just tea and muted talk which I could do without now, but I still felt a twinge of guilt beneath the exhaustion.

You are him exactly.

None of them knew the last time I'd spoken to my dad had been months ago — to tell him I am bisexual. None of them knew that we'd argued, that he said my sexuality was a lie, a Western conspiracy, that I was lost and just needed guidance, that of course he still loved me, 'but son, it's a short step away from bestiality or even paedophilia'. Not the same, but too close for comfort. None of them knew a part of me was convinced I had been the very last thing my father's ailing heart could handle, and that it had killed him.

Attila's room was at the end of a short hallway. There was a handwritten note on the door, but I can't remember what it said. His double bed was perfectly made, not a wrinkle in sight, his blankets and pillows cream coloured, with the Eiffel Tower emblazoned across the former and Paris flowing in italics over the latter. A soccer jersey hung on the wall, along with a torn out page from a notebook which had his training schedule on it. Fifty push ups on Monday, he'd written. I tried to picture him doing it tomorrow, but couldn't. I was sure his body would be too heavy. A large chest of drawers was next to his bed, a small flat-screen TV on top with an Xbox, as well as a number of blue and red glass bottles of cologne and a fat wallet.

I remembered the night before, arriving at Babbanne's flat in Mascot, straight from the airport. Outside, a thousand pairs of shoes were piled on top of each other and inside, the owners of those shoes were crammed shoulder to shoulder in the tiny space to witness an old woman's grieving, or perhaps share their own — it wasn't clear. I staggered through them to get to her, my grieving grandmother, her face a withered peach left out in the sun for too long, everything red and cracked. I can't even begin to describe the volume of shrieking when she saw me, in part because I have his face, and in part because I was the boy who'd got away. The boy she never saw until too late, and therefore loved more than the others, because it was a love delayed, a love accumulated but never spent.

'You, my heart,' she would tell me over and over whenever I saw her. 'You, my heart. Attila, too. Orsun, too. But you, oh my god.' And her eyes would become suns. I know it sounds dumb but you've never seen a woman incandescent like this, and she would lean over and grab and kiss me, smelling faintly of cinnamon. Whenever my uncle Sedat, a forty-something security guard who looked like a soft sad Stallone, heard her say this, he would get crazy-eyed and shout, 'You can't say that, Mum! I'm right here. What about me? What about me?' As the last of her children, the third boy, he always felt left out. And she would shrug, murmuring 'I dunno' in her broken English.

That night, there were no suns in Babbanne's eyes, her

son was gone. Sedat was there, looking as ever like a lost boy, his face and eyes clear as a child's, unable to process anything. 'Your sisters were here,' he said. 'They took your dad's things. Look.' And he showed me the bed my dad died in, perfectly made, not a wrinkle to be seen, and his bedside drawers, all of it empty of him and his things.

Six days after the funeral, I attended another. My friend of more than ten years, a woman only a few years younger than my dad, had also died of a heart attack. Inside the chapel at the crematorium in North Ryde, her daughters and friends told heartfelt stories, sang songs, and played a video montage of her that left most of us in tears. At the end of the service, I stood outside in the bright light of the day, dizzied by the stark differences that separated me and the largely white, Anglo crowd of mourners. I thought of the funeral house where Dad's body had been cleaned, then wheeled out on a gurney cocooned in white cloth like a grey un-butterfly, something that would never bloom. How we'd gathered around it; how Attila's head snapped to the side he'd looked away so quick, blinking away tears; how we all touched the cocoon; how I'd leaned over and kissed Baba's cool forehead, seeing bits of cotton stuffing peeking out of his nostrils. I had been around dead bodies before, but I'd wanted to gag at that detail, the wrongness of it; a blockage where air should be.

He was whisked away into the waiting hearse, placed

in a temporary metal coffin, and taken to the mosque in Auburn. We prayed there; first inside with the community, then outside alone as a family, a row of men and some boys, bowing in front of a tin box wrapped in a green tapestry. We moved in concert to the Mufti's calls, washing it with our silent prayers. *It*, not him. I had the mad urge to drag my dad out of there so it felt real; so he could hear the prayers and see us all. It was a short drive from there to Rookwood cemetery where a freshly dug hole waited. The lumpy cocoon was picked up by a group of men including Sedat, then awkwardly lowered into the dirt. There was — from start to finish — a sense of brisk efficiency, even urgency to it. The sooner he was buried, the better.

There was no song, no series of anecdotes or speeches, the brutal reality of the body was before us the entire time, and it had to be lifted, then lowered, then covered by a mound of red clay chunks. I can still feel the roughness of that earth in my hand as I scattered a handful into the open grave and said goodbye.

A month passed before I could return to Sydney and see Attila again. I'd had to leave for work, and he'd been on my mind the whole time. The one week we had in June was the worst and best of my life; a chance to see him and be part of his world, even though it meant occupying his room and him having to sleep in Sumi's bed. The one thing I wanted the most that week was to see him play soccer, which everyone said he was a star at, and which the trophies in his room affirmed. It didn't happen, of course; though he'd been so ready first to train, and then to play. We were both disappointed in that, for different reasons. Dad had died in his sleep the same morning he was supposed to take Attila to a match. I keep thinking of him in his long shorts and jersey, his boots on, waiting to be picked up. Waiting for Dad that day the way I waited for a lifetime, or at least a childhood, which feels like the same thing.

Now that I was back, I was determined to see him play. I was staying at a friend's place this time, so I had to get up at 6.30 am, shivering in the cold, and get across the huge sprawl of Sydney. I got to the house at 8 am, and was welcomed in by his mother, who I shyly kissed hello. I still felt new and strange around her. Attila wasn't ready yet, and both Sumi and his mum took turns yelling at him to change into his team uniform, and get his boots, while he groaned that it was still early, way too early, they had plenty of time. I sat in the background, simply happy to be there. But smiling too, because Atti — I can call him Atti now, like everyone else — clearly hadn't figured out that Middle Eastern women operate on a schedule half an hour to one hour faster than everyone else and if they tell you to be ready by 8, they'll be in the car by 7.40.

There was a minor catastrophe when Atti realised his jersey had been washed that morning and wasn't dry yet, and suddenly there wasn't any time, we had to be on the road, so Sumi draped the wet jersey over the car window, lodging it there firmly before speeding off, the plum-coloured flag of it rippling in the wind as we drove. It took most of an hour to get there, which is true of any place in Sydney, but seems especially so for suburban sports grounds, which are always in out-of-the-way places surrounded by hills. I had never been the sporty kind, that was the province of my older brother and cousins, but I was still familiar with the shining green fields, the smell of snags grilled outside the cafeteria, the blur of kids in bright colours milling around and, most of all, with the chain-link fence that kept me from the action, forever a spectator.

We had gotten there just in time. I watched Atti greet his teammates, the boys slapping hands, saying, 'What took you so long, bro?'. He rushed off to finish changing into his now-dry jersey. He came out a minute later, and they began a few warm-up exercises on the field, a row of boys in purple trotting up to a line of traffic cones, then kicking their legs to the side in a slow arc before starting the pattern again. It could have been a chorus line, and it was as mesmerising as a dance. Were they limbering up their ankles? I had no idea. I've never had a reason to pay attention to soccer before, and this was the last match of the season, but I was prepared now to make it my new obsession.

My sister Gulsah arrived with her husband and kids in tow. We sat on the sidelines as the game started, my brother-in-law shouting out encouragement to Attila. I ignored everyone, taking about a hundred photos, trying to burn the image of the boy, my brother, the other son, into my mind: his not-yet graceful tallness, his gawky build, the way he seemed to float not run, a little bit aloof from the whole thing. My heart was beating too fast, my mouth dry. It was happening, I was here now, and I wasn't. I kept seeing him at the funeral house, crumpled against the wall crying as the hearse slowly drove away, his sisters and mother crowded around him; how I'd pushed through them, grabbing his stupid puffy jacket to crush him against me; how he'd clutched at me, thin body shaking, tears wetting my cheek; and how strange it was that I had known from the second I saw him through the doorway that I loved him completely and with every cell in my body, this boy I had never really met before.

A whistle pierced the air. There was a smattering of yells from parents, the sun bearing down, there was my nephew holding up a toy plane against the blue sky, and a whole field of sons kicking out at something — a ball, a patch of grass, each other. And just like that, it was over.

AMRA PAJALIC

Amra Pajalic, Melbourne-based writer, editor and educator, was born in Australia of Bosnian migrant parents. She returned to Bosnia to live for four years during her childhood before relocating to Melbourne. This story is a memoir piece about returning to Australia after that time and struggling to acclimate as a high school student in a very monocultural high school. Amra writes, 'It deals with the trials of being bullied against the context of missing out on the usual primary school milestones that would prepare me for the Australian high school experience.'

School of Hard Knocks

The students carried the boy spread-eagled and slammed his genitals against a pole. He dropped on the concrete like a sack of potatoes, holding his crotch, squirming in pain. Sounds that I didn't think a human could produce came out of his throat.

'Bastard just got knackered.' Kayla laughed, noticing my horror. 'Every school tour starts like this.'

Kayla was my new schoolmate and she was giving me a tour of my new school, The Tech, under orders from our year seven homeroom teacher. Her friend Sharon was tagging along and she sniggered too.

Feeling nauseous, I wondered what I would see next as we continued around the school grounds.

'He'll be walking like a cowboy tomorrow,' Sharon said beside us, shaking her brown curly hair. My eyes caught on her Barbra Streisand honker, and it was only when I really focused on her other features that I noticed she had pretty hazel eyes and a full mouth.

'Don't ever wear tracksuit pants to school,' Kayla said. She was the archetypal Anglo girl, tall and skinny, with white blonde hair and freckles.

'Why?' I asked. My new school had a uniform and Mum had bought me tracksuit pants with it.

'Because you'll get *dacked*.' Sharon said. They pull down your trackies and expose your underwear for everyone to see.'

'Or if you wear tracksuit pants, at least wear pretty undies.' Kayla pulled up her dress and showed me her striped blue and white underpants with a white bow in front.

I looked away from Kayla's underwear, feeling my cheeks go hot. While I blended into the very Anglo school with my blonde hair and green eyes, I had an accent. I spoke Bosnian as my first language for four years of my life and always over-corrected my vowels. People often asked me if I was British or South African. My accent proclaimed me an exotic species and I was a hot commodity — the new girl who had arrived in the middle of the school term. Kayla and Sharon had an apostle.

'Oh, my God, she's blushing,' Sharon exclaimed, peering at my face.

'She's so cute,' Kayla said to Sharon as she put her hand through mine.

'Like a little puppy,' Sharon said.

'But you'll have to toughen up,' Kayla said. 'The Tech is not for the faint-hearted.'

The Tech was not our first choice of school. My mother had taken my brother and me back to Bosnia for a holiday that became a four-year stay. When we returned to St Albans, a suburb in the western suburbs of Melbourne, I was twelve-years-old. My mother tried to enroll me in the high school on the other side of the train tracks — it was perceived as the 'good' high school because the punch ups took place off school grounds in the nearby park — but we were told there were no openings. The teachers there suggested that I enrol in grade six and then start year seven the year after. But I refused to go backwards. The education system in Bosnia was much more rigorous and I knew I'd have no trouble keeping up, so Mum enrolled me in a school that was closer to home.

The school was named after the street it faced, but no one ever called it that. Instead they called it *The Tech* after its previous incarnation as a technical college for boys. Most of the classes were orientated towards the trades: sheet metal, woodwork, auto workshop. Then, along with the new female cohort, other subjects were added: typing, home economics and sewing.

There were punch-ons nearly every week, some on the grounds and some after school in the adjoining streets and park. Even teachers weren't immune to being clocked on the job by a belligerent student. Teachers survived by developing a thick skin and ingenious classroom management. Our woodwork teacher got our attention by taking out his glass eye and placing it on the desk. 'I'm keeping an eye on you,' he'd say, to the delight of the kids.

A few days later after I started at The Tech we were in the toilets during recess. 'Shit, I got my rags,' Kayla said from inside the cubicle.

'What are rags?' I asked Sharon who was standing next to me, looking at herself in the mirror.

'Period,' Sharon said. She was used to my naivety and constant questions as I adapted to being in Australia once again.

'I need a tampon,' Kayla called out.

Sharon reached into her backpack and took out a slim, white capsule, passing it to Kayla under the cubicle door. 'You don't know what a tampon is?' Sharon asked, seeing my face.

I shook my head. I didn't even really know what a period was. I had gone to Bosnia as an eight-year-old and had lived with my grandparents for four years while my mother was in and out of hospital. My grandparents were old-fashioned and had sheltered me from adult matters — whenever there was a kissing scene on TV my brother and I had been sent out of the living room to wait in the hallway until it was safe to return. Now I was thrust into the rough and tumble world of adolescence and I was not well prepared.

'You put a tampon inside to collect the blood.' Sharon mimed the insertion of a tampon.

I did my best not to audibly gulp. That sounded incredibly painful. A few minutes later, Kayla came out of the toilet and washed her hands. We walked out of the toilets and down the corridor. We passed by the year nine locker bays and a boy turned and smiled at me. I'd noticed him smiling my way a few times before and I always smiled back.

'I think Jeremy likes you,' Kayla said as she noticed our exchange.

'He's still looking,' Sharon said after she turned to look over her shoulder.

'Do you like him?' Kayla asked.

Even though my body had started blooming — three pubic hairs had sprouted and my breast tissue was tender — I was still unsure if I wanted a boyfriend, and even if I did, Jeremy would not have been a contender. He had brown hair and nondescript features. He wasn't the sort of boy that girls noticed.

'I don't—'

'I'll bet he wants you to be his girlfriend,' Kayla said, cutting me off before I could finish saying that I didn't know if I liked him. We'd never spoken and our only contact had been a few smiles in passing.

'Wouldn't that be great,' Sharon said.

'But I don't know anything about him,' I said.

'He's in year nine and everyone knows him,' Kayla said.

'Did you have a boyfriend before?' Sharon asked.

I shook my head. I had only developed my first crush in

the three months before I left Bosnia for Australia. His name was Samir and he was the smartest boy in my class. All we did was exchange glances and smiles, and when I stopped studying because I knew I was returning to Australia, and couldn't answer the teacher's questions, he moved from the front row to sit beside me in the back and whispered the answers.

'Have you ever kissed a boy?' Sharon asked.

I shook my head again.

'We'll have to fix that,' Kayla said.

I looked at her wide smile with trepidation. I had been shocked to find out that Kayla had kissed her first boy in fifth grade and had already had a few boyfriends, while Sharon had had her first kiss when she was in grade six. Sharon and her boyfriend broke up when they went to different high schools and now she was on the lookout for her first high school boyfriend. In Bosnia, old fashioned attitudes and expectations about female virtue prevailed. A girl was supposed to avoid members of the opposite sex in case she got a bad reputation. I had once returned home from a female friend's house and my grandfather had beat my finger tips with a stick — I could only imagine the punishment he would have meted out for kissing a boy.

That night I went home and searched through the bathroom medicine cabinet until I found Mum's box of tampons. I took one out of the packet and retreated to my room. After locking my door I sat on the bed and took the plastic sheath off the little white capsule. The tampon was smooth and I spent some time tugging on the string at the bottom until I figured out its purpose. After taking off my undies, I spread my legs, held the tampon against my vagina and pushed it in. It felt dry and slightly uncomfortable, but I persisted until my finger and the tampon were in all the way.

I got up and walked around. I couldn't really feel it inside, but the string was annoying as it tickled my thighs. I sat back on the bed and tugged the string to remove the tampon and winced and moaned as the dry tampon chafed against my insides. After I'd tugged it out, I held my hand against my crotch until the pain subsided. When I got it out, the tampon was slightly swollen, but otherwise looked much the same. I vowed never to use a tampon again.

The next day Kayla and Sharon greeted me at the school gates with beaming smiles. They told me that Jeremy liked me and wanted to ask me out. 'So we told him that you like him too. You do like him, don't you?' Sharon asked, noticing my shock.

'Of course she does,' Kayla interrupted. 'She was smiling at him.'

The two of them stared at me as they waited for an answer. I wanted to tell them that I didn't want a boyfriend, but I had already noticed the hierarchy in our little threesome: Kayla was the leader, Sharon her little follower, and I was expected to be the yes girl who went along with whatever they wanted.

I nodded. Maybe it wouldn't be too bad; besides which, it was kind of nice to know that a boy liked me, even though I didn't like him back.

At lunchtime, we gathered in the school courtyard. I was on one side with my girlfriends, he was on the other with his mates. His best friend, Caine, walked over. 'Jeremy wants to know if you will go out with him,' he said.

I nodded.

Kayla, answered for me, 'Yes, she will.'

Caine returned back to Jeremy and gave him my answer. Jeremy smiled and we were nudged together, while our friends formed a crowd and watched. We exchanged awkward conversation. He put his hand around my waist and we acted the part of the happy couple. I'd never been this close to a boy and I didn't know how to stand, or what to say. Soon enough he retreated back to his mates, and I went back to Kayla and Sharon.

'What did you talk about?' Kayla demanded when I returned.

'He asked where I had moved from.' It was slightly ludicrous that I now had a boyfriend who didn't know the first thing about me.

'You know what happens now,' Sharon said. 'Now you have to get on.'

'What's *get on*?' I asked, feeling my heart race in panic. Did that mean he had to get on me? Did that mean we had to have sex?

'That's what we call kissing,' Kayla said.

My panic subsided, but I was still feeling trepidation. Why was kissing called *getting on*? Was it regular kissing or was there more to it?

I was going through a growth spurt and ate multiple times a day, so at recess the next day I bought my favourite meal: a hamburger and chocolate milkshake and wolfed it down.

'Yuck,' Kayla said. 'You're going to have hamburger breath when you kiss.'

I hadn't even thought about the mechanics of my new status or the expectations on me. The food I'd just eaten curdled in my stomach.

At lunchtime, Jeremy found me and we walked hand in hand to the oval, our friends walking behind us. Jeremy took me to the edge of the oval and we stood behind a bush. As Jeremy put his hands on my waist and bent to kiss me I heard our friends on the other side of the bush laughing and talking as they maintained our faux-privacy. I was in a ditch and he was taller than he usually was so I had to stand on tippy toes. As we began kissing, I took my cue from him and opened my mouth and joined it to his. Jeremy's mouth was minty fresh. My friends told me later that he kept a toothbrush and toothpaste in his locker. We imitated a fish's mouth as we mashed our lips together. Every few minutes he tilted his head to the other side and I followed suit by tilting mine in the opposite direction so our noses didn't smack each other's.

After a few minutes I opened my eyes and watched him. He had his eyes firmly closed as he sucked at my mouth. We kissed for so long that my calf began aching and cramping, but at least the discomfort was keeping the boredom at bay.

Kayla walked around the bush and interrupted us. 'Fourteen minutes,' she said, tapping her watch.

Jeremy smiled, satisfied that he'd achieved his personal best. He took my hand and we joined our friends. I felt like I had a clown mouth, our co-mingled saliva coating my cheeks and chin. I surreptitiously lifted my hand and wiped the drool with my sleeve.

'You can't do that,' his best friend Caine said when he spotted me doing it. 'You can't wipe someone's kiss off you.'

I turned red with embarrassment and looked at the ground.

'It's okay,' Jeremy whispered, hugging me tight.

'So how was the kiss?' Sharon quizzed me the next day.

'Wet,' I said.

She and Kayla exchanged a look.

'What do you mean?' Kayla asked.

'My mouth was all wet.' I touched the skin around my mouth and chin.

'I thought he'd be a good kisser because he's had lots of girlfriends,' Kayla said.

'You mean it's not supposed to be like that?' I asked in surprise.

'No.' Sharon shook her head. 'I loved kissing my boyfriend.' She sighed as she stared into space.

'Do you want me to dump him for you?' Kayla asked.

'Really?' I asked, surprised she was so eager considering she'd been so quick to match make.

'Sure. I'm sure your next boyfriend will be a much better kisser.'

True to her word, Kayla went to speak to Jeremy's best friend and gave him the news. The next time I saw Jeremy in the corridor I wanted to run in the other direction, but he smiled and waved at me, letting me know he harbored no ill will. My short-lived romance left me with no negative after-effects, apart from a distaste of kissing.

Jeremy didn't pine for long. Within a fortnight, he'd hooked up with another candidate and this girlfriend stuck around for a while. I developed a new method of repelling unwanted male attention by developing a crush on the most unattainable boy in our high school.

Over time everything settled back to normal, except for my friendship with Kayla and Sharon. Their viciousness was seeping through and since I was the lowest in the pecking order, I was always the one who had to act on their dares and was the butt of their jokes.

A few months later I walked over to Katherine, a girl I considered my friend. Katherine looked at me, waiting for me to speak. I hesitated, not wanting to follow through on the dare to kick her. I glanced over at Kayla and Sharon. Kayla was staring me down, while Sharon looked away.

My leg seemed to move of its own volition and I kicked Katherine in the shin. Katherine's face tightened. I saw betrayal in her eyes. I wanted to apologise and beg for forgiveness, but I knew not to show weakness.

Katherine braced herself on the wall. She lifted her leg back and kicked me back, her chunky black shoe leaving dark marks on my shins. I knew in that moment that I had transgressed. We were both victims of bullying and Katherine was easy fodder. She was pretty, even though pimples covered her face, the white pus oozing out and looking like semen so that she was often taunted with comments like, 'don't you wash your face after getting cum on it?' While Katherine, like me, had to take her licks when they came, she wasn't going to take them from *me*.

Behind me, Sharon and Kayla were giggling, finding my whole performance hysterical. As I slinked back, my shins throbbing and my eyes tearing from humiliation and pain, Kayla shrieked with high-pitched laughter.

'I can't believe she kicked you back,' Kayla said.

'And you took it like a chump,' Sharon said, clutching her stomach as she laughed.

Later that month, Kayla had a birthday party and I felt the familiar spin cycle of trepidation and excitement in my stomach at the thought of spending a night with my friends.

I had never participated in a sleepover and the only reason I could go was because Mum was in hospital and unaware of my plans, and my stepfather had given permission to end my pleading.

When I arrived, the house was full with all of Kayla's friends already in attendance. We spent the night talking, watching movies and eating snacks. Eventually we exhausted ourselves and fell asleep in the early morning.

I woke sometime during the night to a tingly, cold sensation on my skin. I touched my arm and felt something sticky and shrieked with panic. I heard giggles in the dark.

'Shhh, you'll wake my parents,' Kayla said.

There was a click and the lamp beside her bed came on. I blinked my eyes in the bright light and saw that the girls were sitting around me. Kayla held a toothpaste tube in her hand and I looked down and saw the smeared blue streak of it on my arm. I started crying, caught off guard in the state between wakefulness and sleep, impotent rage and sadness filling me.

'Don't be a cry baby,' Kayla said. 'It's just a prank.'

I saw the disgust and embarrassment on the faces of my friends. I had violated our friendship by not being a good sport. 'I'm not crying because of that,' I lied. 'I was dreaming about my Dad and it made me cry.'

Like most female friendships, our connection was predicated on the age-old rituals of secret telling. Soon after becoming friends, I'd confessed to Sharon and Kayla my life story, including my father's death and my mother's medical condition. I had also earned my popularity because I was able to bring friends home during school lunch breaks when Mum was in hospital and my stepfather was visiting her. My friends asked for coffee.

The only coffee my parents drank was Minas freshly roasted coffee that my stepfather ground using a hand grinder. I made them coffee in the traditional Bosnian fashion by spooning six teaspoons in a *džezva*, Bosnian coffee pot, on the stove and served it on a tray with *fildžani*, small demitasse cups. I demonstrated how they needed to drink the coffee by breaking off some of the square sugar cube and placing it in my mouth and then sipping the coffee. Sharon and Kayla followed suit, scrunching up their faces as they tasted the bitterness of the coffee. After that I served English breakfast tea only.

I had learned to bridge the gap between us by concealing my differences and so now as I pretended to cry because of a dream about my father, I felt relief as Sharon hugged me.

'Poor thing,' Sharon said over my shoulder.

I saw Kayla's sour face before hiding my face in Sharon's hair. Sharon took me to the bathroom where I washed my arm and face. I returned to Kayla's bedroom where all the girls rallied around me, and fell asleep feeling comforted and loved.

The next morning we went to a swimming pool. I watched in envy as my girlfriends donned bikinis that emphasised their curvy bodies, while I put on my red and black one-piece suit. We followed Kayla out to the swimming pool and arranged our towels and bags on the green grass beside the pool. We didn't worry about sunscreen and none of us had brought any, although Kayla had brought a zinc tube that she used to draw patterns on our body so that we would have tan line shapes after the day. She drew a smiley face on her stomach, a big heart on Sharon's back, and a star on my thigh.

'All right, let's go in,' she said, and ran toward the edge of the pool, leaping into the air and holding her knees to her chest as she hit the water.

The rest of my friends followed suit, while I gingerly walked to the ladder and slowly submerged myself. Kayla and the girls kept swimming into the deep end, while I clung to the edge. I had learned to swim as a child and could keep afloat comfortably, but I'd had a scare a few months ago when I'd gone to the sea with a family friend. I'd walked into the water, enjoying the feeling of the squishy sand in my toes, and had stepped into a depression, the water suddenly reaching my neck. As I tried to take a step back to safety I'd lost my footing. A wave crashed over my head and I went under, struggling to scramble back to the surface. As I flailed in panic I swallowed water, and the coughing fit sent me back under. I could see the sky above me, but I kept sinking, my hands reaching for something to hold, but there was nothing.

Suddenly arms reached for me and the husband of my family friend carried me out, where I coughed up the water, my throat feeling scratchy and sore. I didn't risk going in past my knees for the rest of the day, and now that I was in the swimming pool I wasn't going to risk going in any further than my waist.

Sharon came to keep me company and we leant our backs against the side of the pool as we talked.

'What are you doing over there?' Kayla demanded, as she swam over from the deep end.

'Nothing,' I said.

'Come over here.'

Sharon went to her, and I took a step toward them, but as soon as the water pressure hit my chest and I struggled to breathe, the familiar panic took hold and I returned to the shallow end.

Annoyance spread over Kayla's face when I didn't obey her command. She smiled and called our friends towards her. I felt a portent of danger and quickly climbed up the ladder and out of the pool. I was lying on my towel, pretending I wanted to get a suntan when they all came and stood around me.

'Let's go.' Kayla grabbed hold of my arms.

The other girls grabbed my other limbs and tried to carry me to the pool.

'No, stop,' I begged. 'Please, don't.'

'Stop being a baby,' Kayla shouted, her face red from the exertion of carrying me.

As I caught sight of the pool edge I fought like a cornered

animal, kicking and pushing them away. I stood and looked behind me. The girls were watching me with anger. Sharon was rubbing her leg where I'd kicked her and Kayla looked down at the drops of blood on her arm where I'd scratched her.

Kayla walked to me and shoved her face into mine. 'Why are you being such a spoilsport?' she demanded.

I was mute, unable to speak from terror. Kayla slapped me on the face, the sound of her palm hitting my cheek with a loud smack. I heard one of the girls giggle from behind us. 'Fuck off, you dumb bitch,' Kayla hissed.

I grabbed my towel and bag of clothes, running to the pay phone next to the change rooms where I called my stepfather to pick me up. He drove me to Kayla's house where her mother let me into the house so that I could collect my belongings.

'What happened?' he asked as he drove me home.

'Nothing. I just got sunburnt,' I lied.

By the end of the year I was worn out by the relentless bullying rained down on me. At my urging, my parents enrolled me in the school on the other side of the tracks.

I saw Sharon only once after I changed schools. We passed each other as we walked in opposite directions on Main Road after school. She made eye contact, by accident, and then quickly looked away. I was relegated to someone she used to know. I walked on, my head high and my back straight.

WENDY CHEN

Wendy Chen is a Sydney-based, Chinese-Australian writer. This story is a work of fiction inspired by Wendy's interest in historical fiction, Chinese cultural traditions and the stories of Chinese-Australian migrants at the time of Federation. Wendy writes, 'Often, the only narrative we're presented with in respect of minorities throughout history is that they were outsiders and victims of exclusion. I was interested in actually exploring their personal experiences, in terms of the resilience of these people throughout the years of the Immigration Restriction Act *in Australia. These stories can give us a new perspective on history, and reflecting on them reveals to us that they are still relevant today.'*

Autumn Leaves

Chinatown, Melbourne
May 1902

When I used to think of my father, the first thing I always remembered was his voice — the gentleness it soothed me with. In the quiet before our herbal store opened, Ba would murmur to himself as he sorted items into their correct jars and drawers. He would patiently explain how to prepare the medicines, instilling me with confidence rather than doubt. And when he shared stories with me before I slept, his voice would become as even as my heartbeat, pulling my mind and breathing with it.

But in the year after he passed away, when I was fifteen, his voice became distorted within my mind. All I had were shapeless possibilities of what he could say, and endless questions which couldn't be answered by the echoes he'd left behind.

Our only photo of him stood on a small, dark brown cabinet, beside our dining table. He wore a dark suit and tie, and stood at the edge of the group pictured — the precious first photo the Melbourne Chinese Association had taken together with their own camera — and his eyes, deep with thought, peered into the distance. I was dusting the frame again when my mother emerged. She'd tied her hair back, and was wearing the same sort of plain jacket and skirt as I was dressed in — this made it easier for us to blend in when we were out amongst other Australians.

'You should finish preparing those herbs before we go, Jing,' she said gently. 'Ah Lam will be here soon.'

I gave her a trembling smile. It would be my first time seeing my father's grave and the cemetery again since his funeral. In some ways, knowing Ba was buried nearby made it easier to go on. Yet, when I remembered how we'd failed him by not sending his body back to his home village, a heavy pain would settle at the back of my throat.

I wondered whether Ma could sense beyond my silence and hear the tremors within me. In her own face I could see the lines of tiredness, and of age — lines which had only deepened since Ba had gone, lines which mirrored the cuts embedded inside both of us. Yet we had kept going — with a different routine, in a darker, emptier household.

Could we still keep going now?

I wove past our spindly chair and dining table — we had little furniture in our cramped flat — and down the stairs into the store.

The metal sign outside was becoming chipped at the

edges, yet the black letters Ba had carefully painted — *Lei Herbalists* — remained bold, proclaiming our presence to the street. Inside, shadowed in the dimness of the early morning, were tightly-packed rows of jars, boxes and drawers. The scents of sweet, earthy and dry herbs seeped out, tangling together in the air around the shelves.

I retrieved the iron boat grinder, the brass scales and the mortar from behind the counter, and placed them before me. There, I measured out the aged tangerine peel, and my hands fell into a rhythm as they pushed the plate-like grinder back and forth. A steady, calming rhythm, as I pictured Ba there beside me. I could almost feel the warmth where his hands had once wrapped over mine, guiding me.

The usual multitudes of people that filed through Little Bourke Street were yet to arise so early, with the dawn only starting to subside. As I finished preparing, checking and packing the last of the herbs, I glanced at the window every time I heard the sound of footsteps and wheels. Finally, I sighed in relief and made my way to the door — the wrinkle-faced pedlar Ah Lam waved to me as he pulled his cart to a stop outside. His black queue of braided hair flapped behind him in the wind, unlike my own short hair, and his eyes reflected their usual cheeriness, whereas I could only force an expression of calmness.

'Do you have all the offerings ready?'

He bowed his head and gave me his usual smile. 'All here

and ready, Jing *mui-mui*. I was sure to put everything aside for you.'

A relief — here were the essentials: the thin yellow sticks of incense, and the *zi bok*: gold joss paper folded into chains of miniature boat shapes, to be sent to Ba in heaven. Ah Lam had brought the other items I'd asked for, too — spirits, and certain sweets Ba had always liked.

I thanked him and began counting out the money for the offerings, only dimly noticing my mother's footsteps as she approached from behind me. As I handed the coins over, it was clear Ah Lam's eyes were probing me more carefully than usual. I looked up. 'What is it?'

'Have you and your mother thought again about leaving?'

There it was. The same question again. The one we'd been asked so often in the past few months. My eyes turned back to the offerings I was holding, and I chose not to meet his gaze. At that moment, I became aware of my mother's presence at the door — she'd silently slipped to my side.

Ma placed a hand on my shoulder and nodded at Ah Lam, her gaze friendly yet defiant. 'We're staying. It's what he would have wanted.'

I fought down the prickles of unease that arose every time my mother gave this answer. I had to trust her, didn't I? It was she who had ensured we could keep the store running after Ba's death. It was she who had organised his funeral when we couldn't return to Hong Kong to bury him at home, and had made sure we'd followed the traditions as closely as possible. It was she who had pushed me to stay strong, when Chinese men around us showed disdain and told us we should be working inside the house, not taking over a man's business.

Yet, like Ah Lam and everyone else, I'd combed through both the English and Chinese newspapers and their reports of day-to-day developments surrounding Federation, tracking what it would mean for us. Since the Immigration Restriction Act had passed in December, I'd heard more conversations of whispered urgency, more people in Chinatown genuinely wondering whether they should go. The focus of the shipping lines whose advertisements appeared in the newspapers had shifted slightly — to cater to passengers who wanted to leave, rather than cargo which wanted to arrive.

For so many, it made sense to leave now that the new law had come in, now that no more of us could come here. *Falling leaves return to their roots*, as the Chinese saying went. Eventually, our people sought to return home — whether this was at death, something we had failed to fulfil for my father — or when the new land we had come to live in wanted us no longer.

In the most deep-seated parts of me, I was also wondering whether that should be true of us.

I looked up at Ah Lam, whose face still had the same concern from earlier. 'You're going, then?'

'Ship next week.'

I felt a pang in my chest — so many of our friends and neighbours were leaving on that ship, taking the two-month journey to Hong Kong. Every departure of someone I knew bit away at me. Chinatown was still a bustle of activity now, but it was draining away. Eventually, how many of us would be left clinging on?

And yet, if we were to leave, the fear would stay with me too. Melbourne was all I had ever known, and I could barely imagine life in a distant land where both soil and sky were unfamiliar.

My thoughts must have shown on my face, because Ah Lam's expression hardened. 'You should reconsider. You know we'll forever be outsiders here.'

I knew the truth of that. Like him, I had watched with horror the first time I'd seen a grocery shop robbed and left almost destroyed, with slurs etched onto the doorway. I saw it in the way they mocked us week after week in the English newspapers. And sometimes, when looking into the eyes of white businessmen passing through the streets, I would sense it too: the way they saw me as *not like them*, as something to expel. But that would only ever last for a moment and fade, to be replaced with the image of Ma sweeping the floors, or Ba packing the shelves, and I would wonder: how could they not understand that we were as normal as they were, that we simply wanted to live, as they did?

Ma waved Ah Lam away then, and placed the offerings

together in a basket. I did a final check of the store before we turned to leave — to visit Ba's resting place, one of the few in the Chinese section of Melbourne General Cemetery.

My eyes swept across Chinatown as we set off. The street was waking with each step we took, its hum building with the sun's passage into the sky. Autumn leaves were scattered across the rooftops, as well as forming trampled layers beneath our feet — a sight which warmed me in the morning chill. We passed by grocery stores, restaurants, and underneath the two-storey shadows of the Chinese Mission Hall — the priest there would always stop me and offer help, especially in the days after Ba had passed away. Children, too, were hanging by the doorways, maybe to squeeze in a game together before their parents chased them inside.

These same sights had called to me when I'd gazed out the window, also in the early hours of the morning, a year ago. For the first few days after my father's death, I'd barely left the flat, or paused to wonder about everyone else who'd known him. When I'd eventually taken a look a week later, however, I'd noticed so many familiar people — friends and customers and patients of Ba's — standing outside in this same, familiar streetscape.

On that morning, the whole street had appeared to be holding its breath. Even the lanterns had fallen still in the breezeless air — as if they too were waiting, with a tinge of hope, for Ba to appear.

To reach the Chinese section of the cemetery, we had to weave our way south. The multitude of crosses, the statues with their bowed heads, and the gravestones of varying sizes formed a jagged landscape of white peaks against the earth: swept with leaves of yellow and orange and red.

Ba and I had never been here together. If we had, perhaps we would have paused and examined the inscriptions on a particularly grand gravestone, or been awed by the statues of mournful-looking angels. Or perhaps we would have simply taken a long, quiet walk together, immersed in the stillness and deep in our own thoughts. On another day, in another life, I may have done this on my own.

Not today, though.

Ma's steps clicked beside me as we proceeded towards a small, fenced-off section of gravestones. Trees spread their fingers over us as we approached, thick with the richness of their autumn finery. The wind swirled past us and I closed my hand tightly around my jacket; otherwise, it was still.

And there it was. Ba's headstone. It was white and curved across the top, and the characters of his name *Lei Jung* were carved into it, along with the dates of his birth and death. Together, my mother and I swept the leaves and fallen branches away.

Seeing the white headstone brought back another memory — the feeling of the rough white linen my mother and I had worn on the day of his funeral. Ba had been dressed in a white robe, too, and white envelopes containing paper money had been placed inside. I'd long seen, growing up, that white served as the colour of mourning, but only when it was my turn had I truly felt the emptiness it reflected: of life scraped blank of colour.

My mother began setting up all the offerings we had brought. Several fruits, the bottle of spirits and the sweets were placed on the sides in the space in front of the gravestone, and a bowl was placed in the centre. She then struck a match and lit three of the incense sticks, which she handed to me.

'You first,' I murmured. My eyes were still fixed on Ba's grave.

My mother stepped to the centre, before the grave, and bowed three times in succession. 'Look after us in the challenging days ahead,' she said. 'And help us to continue helping those around us.' She placed the incense sticks upright in the bowl in front of the grave, and stepped aside for me to come forward.

How can you be so certain, Ma? Why can't I feel that, too?

My eyes flickered to the smoking incense sticks. Long and gold, they reminded me of the pillars of myth, standing at the ends of heaven. Avoiding my mother's gaze, I said: 'How can we keep going, here, without Ba? Especially now?'

It had already been one year, but now — the days would only get harder as they went by. Though many others were yet to leave us, knowing how close they were to doing so was a reminder of how I had felt after Ba's death all over again: alone in a way I hadn't realised it was possible to feel. Alone in a way I didn't want to admit to my mother.

There was a momentary silence, and when I looked up, Ma's smile was warmer than I expected. She seemed to have heard the unspoken question in my thoughts: *How can you be so sure that Ba wanted us to stay?*

'Do you remember this, Jing?' she said. '*Lok jip …*'

'*… gwai gan.*' Here it was again. *Falling leaves return to their roots.* 'I know, Ma. What everyone here wants.' I shivered at the thought of the dead so close to us, potentially uneasy — because their bodies, like Ba's, had not returned home to the land of their ancestors for their burials.

'*But which roots would they choose to return to?*' Ma said with a smile. 'Your Ba said that once.'

There was something she wanted me to understand here — her voice was hopeful, like the encouragement of a teacher whose student was edging towards the correct answer. I looked up at her. 'What do you mean?'

'Your father sought something different from most falling leaves. This …' — I followed my mother's gaze as she turned her eyes back to the gravestone — 'had always been his desire, from the first days of his illness.'

I paused as her words slowly sank in, and when they did so, I staggered with the weight that hit me in the chest. My voice was a tight whisper when I forced it out: 'Ba *wanted* to be buried here? Even though we couldn't afford to go back with his body … it was his choice from the start?'

She spread her arm around my shoulders, nodding in answer.

I turned back to the gravestone, swallowing against the shock coursing inside. My vision blurred as I released the tears, and a rush of memories from his funeral came flooding back. Amongst the smoke and chanted prayers, a young woman from Beechworth, children clutching her arms, had told me of how far Ba had travelled to reach and treat her. The editor of the local Chinese newspaper had spoken of Ba's kindness when his family couldn't afford a remedy they desperately needed. The voices of multiple other friends and customers had ebbed like tides around me, speaking of the conversations with Ba which still lingered with them, despite his parting.

So this was what my father had wanted. I had been so sure of how much we needed him that I'd missed something simple all this time: that he'd needed Melbourne and Chinatown just as much. Everything he'd worked for and envisioned had been *here*, in the adopted homeland where he'd been laid to rest.

Another orange-gold leaf drifted to the ground beside me, joining the clusters which already lay at the foot of the tree. *Falling leaves return to their roots* — I knew the truth of that. But when leaves stray far from the tree, perhaps new roots can be created. These were the roots I'd sprung from, and grown entwined with — and would continue to hold on to, like my father.

When my breathing was steady once again, I bowed before the grave as my mother had, then helped her start the fire that began the burning of the joss paper. From their golden chains, the smoke rose in tendrils — carrying riches to Ba, in heaven.

For that moment, however, he felt much closer. The earth under which he lay quivered beneath me, filled with the richness of his presence. It promised me strength for the days ahead — here in the land that had become a part of us; here in the life we had chosen together.

Author's Note: According to the Chinese Museum in Melbourne, the number of Chinese-Australians declined sharply as a result of the *Immigration Restriction Act* — from around 50,000 in the 1880s to around 9000 in 1940. Throughout those years, Melbourne's Chinatown survived. Few of its residents were women, though there were certainly real figures like Jing and her mother amongst them, who worked in business and were integral to the community. Note, however, that I've used some creative licence in making Jing an only child; this would have been unlikely at the time.

MICHELLE AUNG THIN

Michelle Aung Thin, Melbourne-based writer and academic, was born in Burma and is of a complex Anglo-Burmese (Indian, Burmese, Irish, German and Dutch) heritage. This story is a work of memoir that interrogates the process of negotiating who you are in the context of where you are. Michelle writes, 'I think that you never find answers to questions of identity, belonging, what mobility means to people. But I also think that's the power of writing — it helps you feel and think your way through life's demanding questions.'

How to be Different

I have an accent, and when Australians first meet me, they often want to know if I am American or Canadian. Then, because of my looks, they want to know whether I am part Asian. And then they want to know how long I've lived here, in Australia.

I tell them: *Canadian, half Burmese, half European, and eighteen years in Melbourne.* That's when they finally ask, 'So, do you *feel* like an Australian?'

I know what they're getting at. I just don't know how to answer them.

I lived in London for thirteen years but do I consider myself English?

I grew up in Ottawa and spent four years living in Toronto, but while I still think of myself as Canadian, eighteen years is a long time and Australia is also part of who I am.

I was born in Rangoon, Burma, and I often describe myself as Burmese because that is how I look, with my dark skin and dark eyes, but I don't speak the language and in

Yangon (the new name for Rangoon) nobody thinks of me as anything but a westerner.

If I was being accurate, I would call myself Australo-Anglo-Canadiano-Burmeseo. But I can barely remember all that, let alone say it without running out of breath. Most of the time, I bob along, fitting in and being different, all at the same time. It's only when I think about it, like as I write this, that I stop to ask myself all over again: *What does it mean to fit in? What does it mean to be different?*

The first time I remember asking these questions was back when I was in Grade Two and a new kid, Ashok, joined my class at Blackburn Hamlet Elementary School, in a suburb of Ottawa, Canada. Our teacher, Mrs. Banton, introduced him just before show and tell; a skinny boy with great big, blinky eyes, from a place called Ceylon (which is what Sri Lanka used to be called).

Ceylon, Mrs. Banton told us, was just below India, part of the continent of Asia.

Asia! I thought excitedly. I knew where Asia was because I was born in Burma, also in Asia. And so, because Ashok was from the same faraway part of the world as me, and because I was still relatively new to the school and hadn't found any real friends, I made a beeline for him as soon as the bell went for recess. I introduced myself as we changed our classroom slippers for our rain boots and together we walked out into the playground.

Away from the classroom, Ash was no longer a blinky-eyed, shy kid, but a seven-year-old bad-ass. He told me he was only in Ottawa for a little while and missed his school in Ceylon because of the tricks he and his classmates used to play on teachers — throwing pebbles at their backs, making animal noises in class. 'And when they turn around, we pretend nothing has happened. The teachers are scared,' he boasted.

I was impressed. Our teachers roamed the playground, their heads so high up you could barely tell where they were looking, let alone what they were feeling. I certainly wouldn't throw things at their backs or make animal noises to test them. Ash seemed daring and super cool.

Ash then showed me his best trick. He flipped up his eyelids, exposing the bloody undersides, and rolled his eyeballs back into his head. Painful red-pink eyelids contrasted with bluey-white eyeballs contrasted with dark brown skin. The effect was awesome, like a zombie, or Lurch on *The Addams Family*, my favourite TV show. I went 'eeewwww' in total admiration.

It was the awesomeness that made me careless. Only when Ash was flipping his eyelids back to normal did I realize that we were being circled by the gang. And that things were about to go wrong.

The gang was the de facto authority of the playground. Sure, teachers were on patrol, stopping fights and enforcing school rules, but it was the gang who kept kids in their rightful place. They ruled by the power of social judgement based on taste and an understanding of how things ought to be. They relegated the farmers' daughters and sons from the asphalted centre of the playground to the grassy bits under the climbing equipment, now soggy as winter drew near. They pushed the socially irredeemable out to the perimeter fence, where the water tank and garden shed were. (Incidentally, I'd once licked this water tank in mid-winter because it was pink and frosty and looked like a giant icy pole. My tongue froze solid to the metal tank and I was stuck there for the whole of recess, finally forced to rip my tongue away when the bell went, leaving most of my tastebuds behind.)

Gang members were a microcosm of the new suburb of Blackburn Hamlet, built on what had until recently been farms and before that, First Nation *Odawa* land. They were tow-haired kids with freckled noses who spent their holidays camping, who brought peanut butter and jelly sandwiches to school, or soft squares of cheese individually wrapped in plastic. If you refused to comply with their verdicts, you got a nickname. Like *Stinky Stephanie*, wild-eyed, messy-haired Stinky Stephanie who roamed the very farthest reaches of the cyclone fence. Nobody wanted to be like her, least of all me.

I lived in Blackburn Hamlet, too, in the same suburban crescents, courts and cul-de-sacs as members of the gang, but I never considered trying to join them. I had no idea what going camping was like. My family went on car trips for our vacations, to Montreal and Quebec City and Granby Zoo, staying in motels and taking part in what my mother called the 'Learning to be Canadian' project. I had certainly never tasted peanut butter and jelly together. My parents had peanut butter and onion sandwiches instead, equally disgusting. And my father refused to allow that plastic-wrapped, orange pseudo-cheese anywhere near our fridge. But even though these things seemed glamorous to me, they weren't alien. Canada was all I knew. Burma, the land of my birth, was more of a mystery. It was my mum and dad who needed to learn to be Canadian. I just was.

And yet, I was also different. We had a yellowing clipping from the *Ottawa Citizen*, the local newspaper, on display at home to prove it. It was an interview with me and my mum, and had a big picture of us at the top. We had been interviewed because we were the first migrants from South-East Asia to arrive in the city. The reporter wrote that 'the baby's preferred food is rice!' But, despite that exclamation mark, I had long grown out of loving rice. Apart from the brownness of my skin, I couldn't work out what about me was so very different. I worried that I didn't really know *how* to be different. That was another reason why I was fascinated by Ash and desperate to be his friend. He *knew* what it was like to live in Ceylon, he *was* an Asian. For him, being different was effortless, and a badge of distinction.

It was this distinction that also attracted the gang. The new kid from Ceylon was a novelty and as the rulers of the playground, they should have been the first to hear about the taunting of teachers, to view the zombie-eyeballs trick and to be told where and what Ceylon was so that they could judge it. But instead, I was monopolising him in a way that made it hard for them to break in. On the other hand, Ashok and I were both from the same part of the world so it was logical for us to seek each other out and hang together; it appealed to the gang's sense of order. One thing was certain: recess was short and action was necessary. I could feel the gang debating, making plans, circling until they finally came to rest a few feet away.

Jane, the leader of the day, marched over, and wasted no time in putting their plan into action.

'Did you know your boots are on the wrong feet?' she demanded of me.

This was a genius move. Every self-respecting seven-year-old knew how to tell their left shoe from their right shoe. Except me. Time and time again, my mother would put my left shoe beside my left foot and right shoe beside my right foot. She would trace the outside curve of my left foot with her finger and then retrace that same shape on the outside of the left shoe to show me how they were similar. But as soon as she stopped tracing, I could no longer see the sameness or the difference. Especially not with my lace up shoes, which fit closely to my feet. Not with my white patent leather strappy party shoes either. And definitely not with my black gumboots, which looked identical to each other. Even now, as an adult, I *still* mistake the right gumboot for the left and vice versa. So, when Jane accused me of getting the feet wrong, I didn't even bother looking down as I would have no clue whether or not she was correct.

Mixing up left and right boots was humiliating in another way. When I'd arrived at the school, I'd been surrounded by the gang and interrogated, just as they were about to do to Ash. Who was I? Where was I from? How many brothers and sisters did I have? How many pets? And why was my skin brown? Was I an Indian?

I told them: *Michelle, moved here from the city, one brother, one sister, no pets, and my skin was brown because I was from Burma.*

Burma! Ta dah! I thought they'd be impressed like the reporter from *The Citizen*. I thought they'd ask me questions which I would answer cleverly, earning their lifelong respect. But they weren't impressed, and they didn't ask me questions. Instead, one of the kids pointed out that my boots were on the wrong feet. And rather than admit that I didn't know how to work out right from left, I said, 'In Burma, nobody needs to tell left from right.'

This was not just a lie, but also a mistake. The lie made my stomach clench as soon as I said it. And I paid for the mistake almost instantly because some kid piped up. 'That's right. They cannot tell left from right because they are poor and have no education.'

No, wait, what?

'Yes,' said another kid, 'and they don't have clean water to drink ...'

'... and they live in grass huts,' — a terrible thing in the land of aluminum siding.

The gang kids were speaking with such authority, and I had such limited actual knowledge of Burma, I felt that I couldn't contradict them. If I did, I would just show my ignorance of the place I was born and make things worse. Then came the clincher.

'Your country is backward. That is why you came here. This country used to be backward. Countries take it in turns.'

Backward? Was that what different really meant? Was that what made grass huts worse than aluminum siding?

Of course, I know now that this was totally bogus. If I didn't know much about Burma, then those kids in the gang knew even less. What they were spouting were stereotypes — over-simplifications and generalisations used to define people and places. Stereotypes are what people fall back on when they don't know about something. Stereotypes *feel* like knowledge. But they're not. Knowledge takes effort. You have to try to see things as they are. You have to go beyond the general and the superficial to the specific. You have to seek out or experience things beyond the confines of the everyday.

That is why we were all so fascinated by Ash. He had knowledge of a faraway place, outside all of our experience. This is the power of difference. It was this power I was drawing on when the gang had interrogated me. I had thought I could exploit their ignorance by pretending that the Burmese didn't even know left from right because *I* didn't know left from right. Instead I'd betrayed my mother and branded myself *backward* as well.

So, when Jane asked me if I realised my boots were on the wrong feet, she had me at my most vulnerable. I was embarrassed by the 'backwards' label that I felt I had brought on myself. Worse, Ash was watching. I didn't really know what to do. All I could think of was to simply say, 'Thank you.'

Amazingly, 'thank you' worked. Jane hadn't been expecting that and surprised, retreated back to the gang. But I knew I'd only bought myself some time.

Sure enough, it was only a minute or two before Jane came marching back.

'Well, are you going to change them? Your boots?'

The gang members moved in, keen to hear what I would say.

'Yes.' I replied. But I didn't bend down to do it.

Janet Caster, that day's second in command, stomped forward.

'Maybe she can't change them. Maybe she needs our help.'

I definitely did not want their help. I wanted them to go

away. But it didn't look like they would. I glanced at Ash. Did he suspect he had made a fatal error in going with the first overture of friendship? The gang closed in tighter.

'I *can* change them myself,' I insisted. To prove it, I bent over and started tugging.

The problem was gumboots are not just hard to put on, they're even harder to pull off. Especially if you've got them on the wrong feet. If you're trying to remove them while still standing in them *and* attempting to seem like a worthy person to be friends with, well you have no chance. I tugged hard at those boots but they wouldn't budge. Ash was clearly thinking he'd wasted his zombie eyeballs on me. Finally, Jane and Janet could stand it no longer.

'Let us help you.' Jane bent over and grabbed my right foot (or maybe it was my left). Janet bent over and grabbed the other. They both pulled. I fell over onto my back. There was a cry of alarm from the gang. Pushing people over was exactly what attracted the attention of the teachers. But Jane and Janet were committed. They had to keep going. They tugged harder until, with a sucking sound, one boot and then the other came off. Jane and Janet then exchanged boots and put them on the correct feet.

'Thank you,' I called out, lying there on my back, my feet still sticking straight up in the air. It was my final attempt at dignity and retaining Ash's good opinion. But the gang had already moved on. My Singhalese friend was already in their midst. I heard their collective 'eeewwww' as he flicked back his eyelids to reveal zombie eyeballs.

And then the bell went for the end of recess.

I slunk back to class and then, at lunch, slunk off to the edges of the playground, where I sat alone. Not even Stinky Stephanie would keep me company.

Ash ran with the gang for the rest of that day and part of the next. But the day after, he was sitting on his own at the edge of the playground as well. We glanced at each other, but that was all. Friendship was no longer an option. The whole boot incident had just been too embarrassing.

Fast forward through the rest of primary school, through middle school and high school and all those years of slavish conformity, to university in Toronto: a bigger city and a time of life when being different was what you *wanted* to be because it made you interesting (although it turned out that *interesting* was sometimes just another way to be the same).

Fast forward through London, the biggest of all the cities I've lived in, where what had once been different elsewhere was everyday ordinary on the Tube.

Fast forward to Melbourne, Australia, to Wurundjeri land, and my son's first day at the inner-city primary school near our house. As I stepped through the school doors, my son's little hand in mine, I felt like I was stepping back into Blackburn Hamlet Elementary School all those years ago. It was so similar, except where we had asphalt, this playground was covered with AstroTurf and although there was a shed and a water tank, I knew this one would never freeze over to look like icy poles. Most of the kids had surnames like *Nguyen* and *Chin* but would once have been *Kontis* or *Katsoumis*, and before that, *Brady* or *Byth*.

Fast forward to right now. To me sitting here writing this and wondering what *how to be different?* really means. What do I know now that I didn't when I was trying to persuade Ashok to be my friend?

You have to be different *from* something. That something is a measure. And that measure is often what is 'normal'. Those people who would tell you who you are and where you belong consider themselves, above all else, to be 'normal'. Maybe they like to think of themselves as upholders of normality for there's power in being someone who can say, *you are the same as* and *you are different from*. Yet there is a power in being different too. It is the power of knowledge, of richness of experience. Of being able to see the world from more than one perspective.

ALICE PUNG

Alice Pung is an award-winning author, editor, speaker and educator whose ethnically Chinese parents were born in Cambodia and came to Australia as refugees. She grew up in the working-class Western suburbs of Melbourne in the midst of a terrible economic recession. This story is a work of fiction. Alice writes, 'While many long-standing residents of my area couldn't find jobs, many new immigrants were moving into the neighbourhood because rent was cheap, and this escalated racial tensions. My story reflects on how class alters race relations in a suburb.'

The Last Stop

Funny I'd never considered Asian chicks before, never found them attractive. In fact, Tommo had this half-joke that they were the last stop, as in the last stop before a guy going fully gay. You'd know if one of your mates was heading that way if he started dating an Asian chick, coz they were supposed to have no curves or nothing. My kid sister had made me watch Disney's *Mulan* seven times with her, so I know what I'm talking about.

I'd won the trip to China as a joke. Some interschool competition sponsored by the Rotary Club and the Confucian Society. It was Tommo that saw the ad in the local paper and pointed it out to me. *Win a trip to China. Write an essay about what the teachings of Confucius mean to you. Open to all high school students Year 9 and above.* I'd snickered.

'Confucius say, *Man who go through airport turnstile too fast will arrive to Bangkok.*'

'Go on then, you should enter,' he told me.

So for a laugh, we sat down and punched out a five

hundred-word essay based on some quotes of Confucius that we'd found from brainyquote.com. *It does not matter how slowly you go just as long as you do not stop* was the first quote, and Tommo said it was about me because I took ages to learn stuff. Then when we'd finished, Tommo didn't want to put his name on it, so we put mine down instead.

I'd never won anything in my life. The judges said the voice was *simple in its insight, with a keen awareness of irony and racial stereotyping*. I had no idea what they were on about, but I took it to mean that I didn't write like a tosser, coz the other two essays that also won were full of wanky words like 'ascendant' and 'vicissitudes'. Tommo was so pissed off because he said half of it was his work anyway, but I'd done all the typing while he'd just sat there saying stuff like, 'Now write about the time your dad learned his lesson getting stuck under the bonnet of that Camry he was fixing,' but it wasn't funny coz my dad got some pretty serious burns from that episode.

Anyhow, so what started off as a joke ended up with me going to China for two weeks to Confucius' ancestral homeland in the Shandong province, with a boy named Raymond and a girl named Grace. Mum told me to pack the Imodium in case I got diarrhoea from the spicy food, and Dad told me not to go to any hairdressers coz they doubled as brothels. No one in our family had been to China before, so Dad asked Vo from the auto-repairs, but Vo said he was Vietnamese, and Dad said it didn't matter but could he please give his son some advice. So that's where Dad got the hairdressing warning from. Just to be safe, Dad gave me a buzz cut before I left.

Grace and Raymond, you could tell they were really uptight. They both came from grammar schools, and wore a lot of white and tan during this trip, like walking advertisements for café lattes. He had hair like Sideshow Bob from the Simpsons, except it was cut short and carefully parted in the middle, like fat orange wings to help his big head fly off at any little thing I said. Grace was pretty hot with her pale eyes and floaty hair, but she often ignored me, or pretended not to understand what I was saying. Like, WTF? We both spoke English.

But the Chinese students at the host school dressed exactly like me: tracksuit pants and T-shirts in bright colours. The first time we met, one of the boys came up to me, this staggeringly tall dude — like, monster tall, I didn't even know Asians could be that tall coz the ones in Australia are just squat little packages like Vo — anyhow, he came up and high-fived me. I had to stand on my toes to reach his hand, but admittedly I did feel a bit like a legend. Coz he didn't do it to Raymond.

I thought I would hate it in China, but I effing loved it! Along with some other old Rotary Aussie people, we had a guide named Ziran, who was pretty cool, like a fully Asian Keanu Reeves. They fed us like kings; every night tables with the spinning things in the middle and about twenty plates of food on them, going round and round. I ate everything, while Raymond and Grace praised the food to anyone who was listening but just picked and poked at it in their bowls. One evening, there was a steamy brown meat on the table and I asked Ziran, 'Is this dog?', and Grace looked at me as if I had asked if we were eating foetus, but Ziran said, 'No, it's turtle, is a Chinese speciality,' and I said, 'Oh, cool' and continued eating, but Grace literally gagged, and afterwards she said, 'How could you?' but I could have asked her the same thing because she'd been the one spitting out the food of the hosts into a red napkin.

And another time, when Raymond was rabbiting on in English about *Jin Dynasty* this and *Yuan Dynasty* that to our host students, I blurted out, 'Kooooong Miaoooooooooo!' which means Temple of Confucius in Chinese, where we were visiting, but I said it in a really dramatic kung-fu way, extending the last syllable in a high pitch, like the noise Bruce Lee makes before he kicks you in the balls, and all the school students, all sixty-eight of them, cracked up, and Ziran patted me on the back and said, 'You funny man.' That evening Raymond muttered something to Grace about not letting racist hoons on a cultural tour, but I didn't care because Dan the monster tall basketball bro had asked me to play ping pong with him and they were gunna take me out to karaoke later on, while those other two spent their night writing more speeches about Chinese history to deliver to their bored Chinese hosts.

And the girls! I had thought that Asian chicks were all shy and hard to read, but these Year 10 girls came up to me early on and asked me a whole bunch of questions in English like, 'What says on your T-shirt?' (Billabong), or, 'Do you watch *Friends*?' One of them touched my hair, another pinched my nose and laughed. A third poked me in the stomach and said, 'Heh, so fat!' But strangely enough there was no meanness in any of this, or coyness, or sexy stuff. They'd called me *Pangzi* which I think meant 'Fatty', but I got the feeling that they *liked* my chub.

Anyhow, I ended up spending most of the trip with the Chinese students, since I couldn't stand Raymond and Grace. They'd spent most of their trip with their heads huddled together like a little self-contained satellite unit, talking, talking, talking. 'Cultural capital', 'enlightening experiences', and 'ethnic enhancement' was some of the shit I heard coming from them, but their pricey white runners were always clean and their laughter like little dying splutters down a drainhole.

My Chinese mates and I, we did fun stuff like going outdoor swimming, kite flying and I even taught my basketball bro Dan some footy, which he called 'The Olive Ball' coz of its shape. Grace and Raymond kept to themselves, since I think they hadn't expected the Chinese students to be so *boisterous* (Grace's word for *bogan*, I think). And they kept trying to foist their shitty Chinese onto the students, who all just wanted to test out their English.

I was all teary at the airport before we left, and hugged Basketball Dan and my Chinese bros, and said, 'Wo Men Shi Hao Ping Guo', which I thought meant *We are all good friends*, and they'd laughed at me and whacked me on the back and called me Fatty Apple because what I'd really said was, *We are all good apples.*

When we arrived back in Perth I'd said, 'So long suckers' to Grace and Raymond and didn't hang around long enough to hear them pontificate over my obnoxious self. But when I looked behind me one last time, I saw they were kissing.

Sick.

So anyhow, I was a bit depressed when I returned. Tommo wasn't talking to me anymore because I'd gone on the trip and he hadn't. The new school term had just started, and I had to give a ten-minute talk during assembly about my Rotary cultural tour. I came back as this mini-celeb, but that lasted only a day or so. No-one understood how much I'd *belonged* in Shandong, how those school kids didn't seem to have our bullshit obsession with popularity.

I started googling hot famous Chinese chicks after school because there was nothing better for me to do, and even if there was, there was no-one to do it with. I mean, what Aussie Year 10 would want to go kite-flying? I began to think, man, people here are seriously missing out on good fun. Fan Bingbing popped up on my screen and I imagined her poking me in the belly with one of her red nails. And that Gong Li chick had a great pair of knockers on her, even though she was, like, fifty. The truth was, that old geezer Confucius was onto something, with his sayings about travel, and opening your mind and all that. Because suddenly, I felt more alone than ever and the irony was that I was back at home, with my mum and dad, my school where I played footy, and my old mates (except Tommo).

'You're a bloody bore,' complained Ed one time after school while we were waiting at the bus stop. 'All you ever talk about now is ching chong hot pot.'

'Don't be racist,' I replied. 'It's Chongqing hot pot.'

That's when I noticed her. I wonder why I'd never noticed her before at the bus stop — tall, slouchy, long black hair in a limp ponytail. I was standing close enough that I could see she had a little scar on her chin, which I thought made her look bad-arse in a good way. Maybe she played soccer or something. She was in Year 11 but I didn't know this that day when I turned to her and said hello. When I'd said *Ni Hao* to all those Shandong girls, they'd always said *Ni Hao* right back and giggle and wave. But she told me to go forth and multiply with myself. How up herself! She wasn't even that hot, to be honest.

'You like the Asian girls now?' nudged Ed. 'Remember about the last stop …'

'Don't be a sexist homophone,' I said, and he laughed and laughed but I didn't get what was so funny.

The next afternoon, Ed was away and there were no empty seats on the bus except next to her, so I plonked myself down. I knew her name was Bonnie because I'd heard the plate-faced boy behind us poke her in the shoulder and say, 'Bonnie, heh, *I think he likes you.*'

Ignoring Plate Face, Bonnie stuck her earphones straight into her ears to avoid talking to any of us. I decided she wasn't from China after all, probably just some stuck-up rich international student. **Girls here are cold**, I typed into Google translate, turning it into Simplified Chinese and then messaging it to Basketball Dan through WeChat. **Fatty**, he replied five minutes later, **Return! We miss you. Set you up with a sweet milk tea sister**. Dan didn't need to use a translation program, his English was pretty good, but he appreciated my running everything I typed through Google Translate, because it cracked him up. What the hell was a *milk tea sister*? Was it some kind of sex thing I was meant to get?

Bonnie looked over then, and saw my screen. I covered it up. 'Private.'

'Why are you on Wechat?' she demanded, like the whole of Chinese Messenger belonged to her just because she happened to be Asian.

'Because unlike you, I have friends,' I mouthed.

'Up yours.' She faced forwards, and went back to listening to her Taylor Swift or whatever white-wannabe shit she was listening to.

I couldn't Google 'milk tea sister' on my phone because then she'd see and be down my throat if something weird and porny popped up. So I typed in **what is milk tea sister** and ran it through Google translate, and popped it into Wechat for Basketball Dan. Just at that moment Bonnie poked her nose into my screen again. 'What, you can write Chinese? What the hell?'

'Stop reading my private messages!'

'Hang on.' She took her earphones out and really stared at me then. 'I know you,' she finally said. 'You're that boy who went to China; you won that Rotary competition.' Then she nodded like she knew something about me that I didn't, when I knew that no-one knew sweet bugger all about me now, not even myself.

When I got home, and googled 'milk tea sister' and some smiling girl holding a cup of bubble tea popped up, at first I thought *WTF? This kid looks thirteen, and she's meant to be the hottest thing in China? Sick.* Then I saw more pictures of her on Google images, at the age she was now. Pretty, even with not much make-up on. But the thing that really got to me, that almost made my eyes smart like a sooky mofo, was that except for her weird glow-in-the-dark filtered whiteness, she reminded me so much of that school in Shandong; those girls and guys that had surrounded me every day with their humour and finger-jabbing jibes that were never nasty or loaded.

And I got it — I understood why the milk tea sister was their big thing. She represented something simple, something pure. Something like friendship that could blossom into romance — hooking up was not the first thing you thought about when you saw milk tea sister, but having a laugh, getting teased by her, having your ear pulled, her kicking your arse at PE and gloating over it.

A few afternoons later, I'm sitting by myself and this time I'm on the bus first, and who should sit next to me but Bonnie, when there were lots of empty seats around. I ignored her and looked out the window. Just because I went to China didn't mean she had the right to think I'd been hitting on her.

My phone pinged with a message. I didn't check it because I didn't want her snooping over my shoulder like last time.

'What makes you think I can read Chinese?' she asked, as if she'd just read my mind.

'Umm, I dunno, maybe the way you almost broke your neck trying to read my messages last time.'

'Well, I can't.'

'You Thai or something?'

'No, I'm Chinese.'

'Yeah, but you were born here, right?'

'No. I was born in China. I came here when I was two,' she said. 'My parents sent me to Chinese school every Saturday until I was fifteen, and I learned sweet eff all.'

'Yeah, those Chinese characters, they're a bit tricky. After a while, they all start to look like Arnold Schwarzenegger's signature, hey.'

Bonnie actually cracked up over that.

'I miss China,' I sighed. 'Everyone loved me there.'

'Well, yeah. I don't know how that feels,' she replied. 'Because you know — people don't generally like the Chinese here. We're either fake refugees or millionaires set to take over the city skyline.' Then she said, 'I guess it must feel good. Being among your people, and that.'

I didn't know if she was taking the piss out of me, like she thought I was one of those white kids who thought they were true gangsta because they listened to rap and had one black friend. Except, of course, in my case, substitute black with Asian.

'Maybe I should go back.'

It was then that I realised she was talking about herself.

'Nah,' I replied. 'You're good here.' I turned to look at her, but quickly, like I was just glancing instead of fully checking her out.

'Do you have *a thing* for Asian chicks?'

Would she think I was a creep if I told her about the milk tea sister? Those girls in China had treated me like an equal. They were affectionate in their poking, their laughter was genuine. And the guys, they'd all thought I was cool as, because I'd looked like a fat Ed Sheeran; which is to say, a new and improved version of an old favourite.

'I don't know,' I answered honestly.

To my surprise, she didn't yell at me. Most of the kids were off the bus by now with only a few insignificant Year

8s left. We sat in silence for a bit. 'Heh,' I suddenly blurted out. 'You know, during our trip, there were these two white kids, Grace and Raymond, who had clearly been learning Chinese before they arrived. On the plane there I felt so ignorant. They opened their Lonely Planet Guidebooks and pointed places out to each other, and talked about cultural taboos and shit. They talked as if I wasn't there, because they thought I was a feral. Anyhow, during the whole two weeks, those two didn't even end up visiting the places they'd flagged with post-it notes in their guidebooks. They were horrified they were spending two weeks in a shitty little state school filled with kids who wore tracksuit pants, who were obsessed with *Game of Thrones* and *Prison Break*.'

'Oh I see,' said Bonnie. 'They expected *real Orientals*.' She snickered in a way which I quite liked.

'This is the last stop,' said the bus driver.

'Do you like *Game of Thrones*?' I asked her as we got off the bus.

'This isn't your stop is it?'

I'd missed it ages ago.

'I'll get the bus going the other way back,' I replied.

'Are you following me home?' she accused.

'Nah,' I stammered, suddenly without a clue about what I was even doing. 'I mean, I'll walk you home. If you want.'

'You can't,' she told me.

'What?'

'You can't walk me home.'

Unbelievable! Because we'd been having such a good chat, this really pissed me off. What a princess! I was about to tell her that this was a free country and I could walk down any footpath I wanted, but there was just something about her tone that made me not dare. Something that told me that she was hiding something, like the punchline of a joke.

'Why not?'

'If my parents see me walking back with a guy, they'll murder me.'

'Why, what's wrong with me?'

'Not you specifically. Just any guy. Any random stranger over the age of eleven. They don't trust anyone. They're crazy strict. They'll kill you too.'

I laughed. She was funny, staring at me with those big unblinking eyes. Until I realised she didn't seem to be kidding.

'My dad's got this weapon,' she said. 'He made it by tying a cleaver to the end of a broom handle.'

Now this chick sounded really crazy. I regretted getting off at her stop.

'What kind of person makes this sort of thing?' I exclaimed.

'We own a milk bar,' she said defensively. 'People come and steal things.'

'But that's no reason to make an illegal medieval battle axe!'

'He's never used it,' she said. 'It's just there to keep us safe.'

I told her that I didn't realise owning a milk bar was as dangerous as, say, having a partnership in a Triad-owned nightclub.

'You think you know everything don't you?' she retorted. 'Just because you won that trip to China, now you think you have this secret knowledge about all things Chinese. Well, sorry to tell you this, Caucasian Kongzi, but you know sweet eff all about what it means to have morons come up to you and do the slanty-chinky eyes thing with their fingers, to have kids pretend to speak your language going 'ninnongnang' in the yard, to be called "the last stop" …'

My face burned with embarrassment.

'To have hooligans pinch things every week from your dad's shop, bluntly saying, 'It's fair game, youse steal our jobs, so we steal from youse,' and to have them drive by and chuck rocks through the window so huge that the glass breaks and hits you in the chin so bad you need stitches.'

I really couldn't look at her then. Coz if it hadn't been for me winning that trip, I knew in a few years' time I would consider it a hoot to drive by with Tommo to scratch the new Toyotas of the Asians in our neighbourhood, coz Tommo told me that the government gave reffos new cars but hardworking Aussies like us had to suffer with second-hand Fords.

In fact, the angrier Bonnie got, the more she reminded me of me. She was bumbling, and awkward, and even stuttered a bit. I knew what it was like to feel that sort of burning, powerless rage. Yes, I had returned to my usual crappy life, but I now suddenly realised that things weren't that much better for Bonnie. She was just better practised at being invisible, but no matter how hard she tried, she could never fully hide from people like Tommo and me.

I was really scared that she was going to cry now. 'I'm sorry your dad's shop got windowed. That's real shit.' I hesitated before I blurted this out: 'But the scar on your chin, it makes you look real bad-arse.'

She stood straighter, and stared right at me. 'I know,' she said, looking pleased.

'Well, if I can't walk you home, I guess I'd better cross to the other side and wait for my bus.'

'Okay.' She gave me a little wave before she turned around and walked down the street. 'I'll see you tomorrow then.'

It was a full half-an-hour before the next bus came, and there was barely any shade on the footpath. The last stop was just a pole with no shelter, but somehow, I didn't mind the wait.

REBECCA LIM

Rebecca Lim is an illustrator, lawyer and acclaimed author,
who was born in Singapore of ethnic Chinese parents. She
migrated to Australia as a child in the early 1970s and
has lived across rural and urban locations in Queensland
and Victoria. This story is a work of memoir. Rebecca
writes, 'Even in 2018, it's extraordinarily difficult to find
Own Voice migrant and refugee narratives in published
Australian literature for children and young adults. I believe
the invisibility of intersectional and marginalised stories in
western society has contributed to the devastating depletion
of empathy in modern life and the entrenchment of systemic
bias. My piece tries to articulate what it feels like to be without
privilege, without language, in a new and contested country.'

Border Crossings

I've always imagined that when you're born, you inhabit
your own wordless island.

You're just a creature of pure sense and feeling, a
participant, not a player; simply acted upon.

Sure, almost 400 years ago poet John Donne might have
said:

> No man is an Iland, intire of itselfe; every man
> is a peece of the Continent, a part of the maine*

But he could think this, and say this, because he was a
connected white man with ties to the English clergy, the
English parliament and King James I of England.

I don't think most intersectional people who live in the
west — people who are routinely marginalised because they
are affected by systemic injustices (such as racism, sexism,
ableism, homophobia) multi-dimensionally — usually feel

---

* MEDITATION XVII, Devotions upon Emergent Occasions (1624)

part of the main: those people, gate keepers or institutions that make up mainstream political, educational, cultural and sporting life.

George Orwell's pigs once declared that all animals are equal but some are more equal than others and I think that's true of the Australian *main* as well; society will be tailored for you — it will be easier, more usable or more understandable for you — if you're the 'right' gender or ethnicity, have the 'right' cultural or religious affiliations, or you are physically, physiologically or neurologically 'normal'. But those who aren't the 'right' ones, including those from whom this land was stolen, will struggle to see themselves in our Houses of Parliament, our sporting teams, our movies, TV, plays or books, our public structures and institutions. Certain overt and implicit privileges are the birthright of some in this nation who identify with its colonisers, but not all. Ironically, those comfortably within 'the main' don't usually see or understand this. They might simply shrug and say: *Well, it is what it is.*

Bear with me as I try to articulate what it feels like to be without privilege, without language, in a new country.

I was born into an extended ethnic Chinese Singaporean family that spoke Hokkien and Mandarin on one side, and Teo Chew and Mandarin on the other. Both sides spoke Cantonese, as well as a passable amount of Malay, so I imagine that during my early days on, let's call it, 'The Island of Sensory Feelings', those were the languages and cultures I was absorbing, the languages and cultures that were crossing the porous borders of my nation of one, before I could even speak.

Then, as I absorbed all the sensory feelings, my island began to split into an archipelago of other islands. The island inhabited by my beloved paternal grandmother who worked three jobs in post war Singapore to feed her six children, for instance, who spoke to me in Hokkien and cooked me Hokkien delicacies; the island inhabited by my forbidding maternal grandparents who barely spoke to me at all, but did so, if moved to do it, in Teo Chew. When I could move off my island, I could step onto theirs and onto others linked to me by blood or friendship, culture or language or daily familiarity.

For me, different local languages and cultures were the sites of all first border crossings, all forays into the territorial unknown. When my father and then my mother — as was the custom in those precarious days — left me with extended family in Singapore as a baby to make a new life for us in Warwick, Queensland, in the early 1970s, their islands winked out of existence for the space of several (possibly confusing) months and new island connections were formed, new borders crossed.

When I was flown to Australia on the lap of my paternal grandmother, not only did I find myself physically on a new island, a contested land, but also in a new realm of culture and language without any linkages to any known archipelagos.

Some, like my Chinese-language educated parents, cross physical and metaphysical borders to come to this country because they choose to. Others do so because they are forced or impelled to by circumstance. Unless you've been living under a rock, just about everyone in Australia knows this. And yet many of us harden our hearts, or turn a blind eye, to those who have crossed those physical and metaphysical borders just to be here. And the very worst of us tell these people — who have left the known behind, who may arrive without language, without friends or any point of real bearing and who may have endured the worst atrocities a human being can face — to *Fuck off back to your own country*.

I see my life in this country as a series of new islands, new playing fields; all constantly shifting, occasionally startling.

Resolutely raised in a Mandarin-speaking household that insisted on a weekly visit to Melbourne's Chinatown for a meal and groceries, I recall spending my entire first year of kindergarten in silence as I desperately worked out what the coloured tin bowls and cups were for (cut apples and milk), why it was bad when kids wet their pants (the blonde teacher lost it and sent them home) and what being asked to sit on the grey oblong of carpet meant (story time). I supplemented my puzzling sessions at kindergarten with learning English from re-runs of *Skippy* — starring a talking kangaroo — *The Aunty Jack Show* — which inexplicably featured a hirsute, moustachioed, singing transvestite in a Victorian-style gown and boxing gloves — *Countdown*, televised VFL matches and endless repeats of the ABBA *Arrival* album given to us by a white Australian boyfriend of my father's female cousin who was studying in Australia.

I didn't feel like a 'right one' in the 1970s when Asians clustered together socially for safety and were the butt end of fatuous word jokes, and I never felt like a 'right one' in the 1980s when little kids who were perceived as weak or different at my school were being shoved into lockers or toilets by big burly Caucasian girls who wouldn't otherwise speak to them. Somehow I managed to parlay all that *Countdown*, *Aunty Jack*, ABBA, *Skippy* and social manhandling into a law degree and working life that gives me access to 'privileged' islands and playing fields — like courts of law and corporate boardrooms — that were probably never made, tailored or intended for people like me.

I've written before about how intersectional women like me rarely think of ourselves in terms of 'privilege'. We might be 'lucky' enough to be able to occasionally access privileged playing fields by virtue of our training or employment.

But we are not necessarily welcomed there, nor are we synonymous with those privileged jobs, situations or places. Even after all these years of speaking and working in English, I still wonder how the sole ESL kid in the kinder class, who could never pronounce the words *hypotenuse* or *hyperbole* properly, got here. The sense of dislocation, distance, separation, sheer impostorship, still sometimes flashes up; is still jarring. That sense of being at a slight remove from everything around me — I don't think that will ever go away. I am always outside, even when I am 'inside'.

The old islands are still there. But they are distant in more ways than mere physical distance — the linkages have corroded. I have forgotten the words, the signifiers and signals, the customs. To my Singaporean relatives I am *huá qiáo* or *huá rén*: a person of Chinese heritage living *abroad* or *away*, cut off from my original islands by all the accretions piled upon me by my life in the West.

I am not a 'whole' creature in relation to any of the languages I speak nor any of the cultures I live in or move across now — no longer fluent in Chinese dialect, I will always *look* Chinese; relatively fluent in English, I will never pass for the white person I sound like over the phone. (*Is that Limb with a 'b'? No, it's Lim without a 'b'*.)

I have an aunt with frontal lobe dementia who is losing the ability to communicate. She is moving out of the realm of speech and facility with English, back through the realm of facility with Chinese dialect into the realm of pure silence and immobility. She is undergoing a kind of casting off, or recession, from the outlying islands of her adult life in Australia back through the islands of her childhood in China. She is returning to her own *Island of Sensory Feeling*, the first island.

Perhaps, John Donne should have said: *Every person is* islands.

We are the sum total of all the islands and playing fields we have taken upon ourselves, like Atlas, like tortoises, throughout our lives. The intersectional in the west, in a sense, are more *island* than those that inhabit *the main*. To simply survive in the west, we must sometimes do more, suffer more, *be* more (at what cost?), just to be recognised, just to live.

Contributor biographies

Graham Akhurst is an Aboriginal writer and academic hailing from the Kokomini of Northern Queensland. His creative nonfiction and poetry have been published widely. Graham received an Australia Council Grant for the creation of new work to complete his debut novel *Borderland*, which will be published with Hachette in 2019. Graham was valedictorian of his graduating year and completed his writing honours with a first class result. He is currently enrolled in an MPhil of Creative Writing at the University of Queensland with an APA scholarship, where he is also an Associate Lecturer in Indigenous Studies.

Michelle Aung Thin was born in Rangoon the same year as the coup d'état (1962) and brought up in Canada; she now lives in Melbourne. *The Monsoon Bride*, her first novel, was shortlisted for the Unpublished Manuscript Fellowship of the Victorian Premier's Literary Awards 2010 and is the product of her PHD in creative writing under the mentorship of Brian Castro. She is the 2017 National Library of Australia Creative Arts Fellow for Australian

Writing, supported by the Eva Kollsman and Ray Mathew's Trust. She is writing her second book, which is about returning to Burma, the country of her birth. She currently teaches at RMIT University.

Wendy Chen is a Sydney-based writer who has appeared as an artist at the Emerging Writers' Festival, National Young Writers' Festival and Noted Festival. She is a co-host of the book blogger collective Lit CelebrAsian, and has been a subeditor and contributor for the literary magazine *Pencilled In*. She has a particular interest in diasporic stories and historical fiction. Find her on Twitter @writteninwonder.

Kelly Gardiner writes historical fiction for readers of all ages. Her latest novel is *1917: Australia's Great War*, recently shortlisted for the NSW Premier's Young History Prize and the Asher Award. Kelly's previous books include the young adult novels *Act of Faith* and *The Sultan's Eyes*, both of which were shortlisted for the NSW Premier's Literary Awards, and *Goddess*, a novel for adults based on the life of the seventeenth-century French swordswoman, cross-dresser and opera singer Mademoiselle de Maupin. She teaches writing at La Trobe University. Kelly is also the co-host of Unladylike, a podcast about women and writing.

Rafeif Ismail is a third culture youth of the Sudanese diaspora. Rafeif sees all forms of art as mediums for change and is committed to creating accessible spaces for young people of marginalised backgrounds in the arts. She is the winner of the 2017 Deborah Cass Prize for writing with the story 'Almitra Amongst the Ghosts'. Rafeif's short story 'Light at the End' was published in the anthology *Ways of Being Here* (Margaret River Press, 2017). She is committed to writing diverse characters and stories in all mediums, is currently working on her first novel and hopes to also one day write for screen. She can be found exploring twitter
@rafeifismail

Jordi Kerr is a writer, youth literature advocate, and support worker for queer young people. Their thoughts about books have appeared in such places as *Archer*, *Books+Publishing*, *Kill Your Darlings,* and *Crikey*. They were a recipient of one of the Wheeler Centre's Hot Desk Fellowships in 2017, and they've worked as a judge for the Victorian Premier's Literary Awards, and the Aurealis Awards. Their favourite book awards, however, will always be the Inky Awards, which are judged by Australian teens.

Ambelin Kwaymullina is an Aboriginal writer and illustrator who comes from the Palyku people of the Pilbara region of Western Australia. She is the author/illustrator of a number of award-winning picture books as well as the YA dystopian series, *The Tribe*. Her books have been published in the United States, South Korea and China. Ambelin is a prolific commentator on diversity in children's literature and a law academic at the University of Western Australia.

Ezekiel Kwaymullina is from the Palyku people of the Pilbara region of Western Australia. He is an author of picture books — most recently *Colour Me*, illustrated by Moira Court (Fremantle Press, 2017) — and novels for younger readers.

Mimi Lee is an emerging writer who was born in Sydney, but spent the majority of her childhood in Shanghai, China. She is a follower of Jesus, and a university student who often wishes her textbooks were thinner. Other than writing stories on themes that are close to her heart, she enjoys reading, singing, bushwalking and watching movies, and is currently praying that her novel manuscript will be published. Say hi on Twitter @MimiR_Lee.

Rebecca Lim is a writer, illustrator and lawyer based in Melbourne, Australia. Rebecca is the author of eighteen books, most recently *The Astrologer's Daughter* (A Kirkus Best Book of 2015 and CBCA Notable Book for Older Readers), *Afterlight* and *Wraith*. Shortlisted for the Prime Minister's Literary Award,

INDIEFAB Book of the Year Award, Aurealis Award and Davitt Award for YA, Rebecca's work has also been longlisted for the Gold Inky Award and the David Gemmell Legend Award. Her novels have been translated into German, French, Turkish, Portuguese and Polish. She is a co-founder, with Ambelin Kwaymullina, of the *Voices from the Intersection* initiative.

Kyle Lynch belongs to the Wongi people of the north-east Western Australian goldfields region. In 2014 Kyle starred in the film *Wongi Warrior* (2014). Most recently, Kyle took part in the 2017 Kalgoorlie Youth Project 'Guthoo: We are One'.

Olivia Muscat has just completed her Bachelor of Arts at the University of Melbourne. She majored in creative writing and Italian and is currently contemplating her next move. She occasionally blogs about life with her guide dog, Jemima, and spends her days reading, writing, and imagining her life as a musical.

Amra Pajalic is an award-winning author, an editor and teacher. Her debut novel *The Good Daughter* (Text Publishing, 2009) won the 2009 Melbourne Prize for Literature's Civic Choice Award, and was also shortlisted in the Victorian Premier's Awards for an Unpublished Manuscript by an Emerging Writer. She is also the author of a novel for children *Amir: Friend on Loan* (Garratt Publishing, 2014) and is co-editor of the anthology *Coming of Age: Growing up Muslim in Australia* (Allen and Unwin, 2014) that was shortlisted in the 2015 CBCA Book of the Year awards. Her memoir *Things Nobody Knows But Me* will be published by Transit Lounge in 2019.

Alice Pung is the award-winning author of *Unpolished Gem, Her Father's Daughter* and *Laurinda,* and the editor of *Growing Up Asian in Australia* and *My First Lesson.* Her latest book is *Writers on Writers: John Marsden,* and she is an Ambassador of Room to Read, the 100 Story Building and the Twentieth Man Foundation.

Melanie Rodriga is a film-maker and academic. She has directed and executive produced eight feature films, the most recent, 'Pinch', won the best film at the 2015 WA Screen Awards. She has a PhD in screen from Murdoch University, is currently embarking on an MA in Literature and is working on a queer YA novel.

Omar Sakr is an Arab-Australian poet whose work has been published in English, Arabic and Spanish. His poetry has or will soon feature in *Griffith Review, Meanjin, Island, Overland, The New Arab, Mizna, Antic* and *Circulo de Poesia.* He has been anthologised in *Best Australian Poems 2016* and *Contemporary*

Australian Poetry, and his debut collection *These Wild Houses* (2017) was shortlisted for the Judith Wright Calanthe award. He is the poetry editor of *The Lifted Brow*.

Ellen van Neerven is a Yugambeh writer from South East Queensland who now lives in Melbourne. She is the author of the poetry volume *Comfort Food* (UQP, 2016) and the fiction collection, *Heat and Light* (UQP, 2014) which won numerous awards, including the 2013 David Unaipon Award, the 2015 Dobbie Award and the 2016 NSW Premier's Literary Awards Indigenous Writers' Prize.

Yvette Walker is an Australian writer of Irish ancestry. Yvette has a BA (Honours) and a PhD from Curtin University. She was a writing fellow at Varuna, the Writer's Centre, in 2009 and again in 2011. Her debut novel, *Letters to the End of Love* (UQP, 2013) won the 2014 WA Premier's Book Award (WA Emerging Writer) and was shortlisted for the 2014 NSW Premier's Book Award (Glenda Adam's Award for New Writing). Her short fiction has been published in *Review of Australian Fiction* and *The Nightwatchman*. Yvette is currently working full time on her second novel.

Jessica Walton is a picture book author, teacher, parent, daughter of a trans parent, and proud queer disabled woman.

She wrote *Introducing Teddy: a story about being yourself* to help explain gender identity in a simple, positive way to her kids. *Introducing Teddy* began as a Kickstarter project, but has now been published in the United States, United Kingdom and Australia by Bloomsbury. It has also been translated into nine other languages. Jess lives in Pakenham, Victoria with her wife, kids and cat.